LUNA MOON DANCE

Fire Jaguars 2

Nicole Dennis

MENAGE AMOUR

Siren Publishing, Inc.
www.SirenPublishing.com

A SIREN PUBLISHING BOOK
IMPRINT: Ménage Amour

LUNA MOON DANCE
Copyright © 2013 by Nicole Dennis

ISBN: 978-1-62242-994-3

First Printing: April 2013

Cover design by Christine Kirchoff
All cover art and logo copyright © 2013 by Siren Publishing, Inc.

Printed in the U.S.A.

PUBLISHER
Siren Publishing, Inc.
www.SirenPublishing.com

DEDICATION

For everyone who loved my Fire Jaguars, here are more kittehs for you to adore.

LUNA MOON DANCE

Fire Jaguars 2

NICOLE DENNIS
Copyright © 2013

Chapter 1

Two pairs of strong hands caressed every inch of her body as Melinda knelt between the powerful males on the expansive bed. The sheets were soft under her knees. Her body tingled from all their attention. She leaned back against one broad chest, arched her back, and thrust her full breasts out for a pair of hands to cup and hold them while nudging the taut nipples. Melinda moaned under the dual attention as wetness dripped down her thighs from her drenched pussy. Oh, she was so ready to be taken by these males, these powerful jaguars.

Lifting a hand behind her, Melinda felt for the soft, long hair of the man. She then held out another hand to touch their third partner. Instead of finding them, the delicious wet dream disappeared. Dressed in bloody scrubs, she stared down at the body of a beautiful, beloved dog that had been crushed under the wheels of a car. The dog panted and whined for her to help him, but she couldn't. There was nothing more she could do other than help him slip into sleep and a journey for the Rainbow Bridge. Blood welled between her fingers, and Melinda tilted her head back to scream in disgust for the senseless tragedy.

The harsh turn of the sensual dream into the nightmares of the particular rough evening during the long shift at the veterinary clinic yanked her out of sleep with a breathless scream. As well as losing one case to the hit-and-run accident, she helped a sweet feline leave her family after the ravages of cancer became too much for the cat and her family. There were times when Doctor Melinda Evans Hurst, MD, DVM hated her job. She tossed and turned in her bed. She groaned, opened her eyes, and shoved a hand into pale white-gold hair. Sitting up, she dragged her hand down her face. These restless nights after horrible days where nothing seemed to go right for the animals were the absolute worse, and she hated them with a passion. If only she stayed deep in the first dream instead of being tugged to the nightmare. She pulled her knees up to her chest. Rolling her head back and forth, feeling the taut muscles of her neck stretch, she glanced at the clock.

Wee hours in the asshat morning.

"Ahh, to hell and back, sweet Goddess, would you please let me sleep? Damn insomnia. Please bring back those hot males to pleasure me back to sleep," Melinda muttered with a groan.

It was the sixth time she dreamt of those males. They were always there, tugging at her dreams with such sensuality. She heard of mates who dreamt of one another before meeting and discovered they were true mates, destined to be together. Could these two males be her mates? Still, she never heard of a triad mating. They were powerful, unusual, and supposedly rare. Could these males be part of the Fire Moon Clan, who lived in the nearby valley where she applied to become a member? Were they so close to her, but still out of reach?

With so many questions, and knowing there would be no more sleep, her inner feline rose forward inside her. She felt as her jaguar stretched in her mind, paced around, and pawed to be released. She knew her jaguar was emotional from the passion the males built inside her body and ached for the losses of the beloved pets. She didn't have the ability to save the precious lives and share her strength with the weakened souls. Now her cat ached for a change and a run through the forest.

Deciding to give in to her cat, Melinda rose from her bed, tugged off the pale-pink nightie and panties, and slid her arms in the simple green silk robe. She gave the ties a loose knot, easy to undo later. Leaving her bedroom, she went to the back exit of the apartment located above the veterinary clinic, which she rented from the other vet who owned the clinic. Nibbling on her lower lip, Melinda raced down the outer staircase.

Downstairs, standing outside the backside of the clinic, where the kennels were kept, her sharp hearing picked up some soft, mournful cries from the six dogs and four cats staying in the clinic. Some were there as boarders while their human families were away from home, while others stayed overnight under care and supervision of a different night technician and nurse.

Knowing the animals would be cared for during her unexpected pre-dawn run, she glanced around once more, sniffed the air to see if anyone strolled about, and pushed off from the bottom step. Reaching the tree line, she crouched next to a fallen tree and pulled off the robe. She rolled and tucked it inside a familiar hole where she would cover herself with the robe again after her run. Another glance and sniff to make sure no one was nearby to watch her change, she called upon her inner jaguar and let her come forward.

The natural magic and gift built within her bloodline, a line she knew nothing about due to her adoption, began to change her body. Five years after her first shift, she continued to hide her changes from the rest of her home clan, the Vernal Moon Clan. It was a secret she tried to keep from the elders and her parents until the High Alpha found out and forced her decision to flee.

The way the Alpha looked at her and wanted her, it kept her from mentioning the truth about what happened when she applied to become a full member of the local Fire Moon Clan. She didn't say a word about her unusual coloring. Since she hadn't received word about her application status, she ended up taking the job and apartment with this small clinic outside the valley.

The shift overtook her human reasoning and thinking before a feline cry escaped into the early morning hours and across the looming mountains. Bones lengthened, cracked, and reformed. Her nose and mouth stretched forward into a muzzle as her eyes moved out. Her pupils remained circular, but a golden tinge altered her natural blue-green irises. Her ears lifted to the top of her head and turned into the familiar triangular ears. Her tailbone grew into the thick tail, which was almost four feet long. Her pale hair disappeared as her skin rippled and flowed over the growing, changing muscles, and lush fur covered her entire length.

Soon, a cream-colored jaguar with soft-gray rosettes and markings leapt and bounded through the trees. Strong, sure paws landed, and claws dug in and pushed off rocks and other natural barriers. She climbed the mountains surrounding the Fire Moon Clan's gorgeous, expansive valley within the Cascade Mountains outside the borders of small town of Paisley, Washington.

Racing away in this natural feline form, all memories of the aching pain, the horrific injuries, and the tears of pets and owners left her mind. Still, her jaguar kept the memory of her possible mates, not wanting to forget them. When she reached a clearing, she turned in a circle.

Assured no one was around, especially the patrolling guardians from the clan, she arched backward and stretched out her front paws. Long, dangerous talons flicked out and dug furrows into the ground. With her butt in the air, the elegant tail flicked back and forth down to the tip. She then reversed position, stretched one back leg out to the paw, and then the other one.

When the stretching finished and muscles warmed, she dropped and rolled around on the ground covered with leaves, pine needles, crushed grass, and dirt. She scratched and rubbed all scent of human from her fur. Another movement had her on her belly, grooming her paws, while her tail flicked back and forth in contentment of the peacefulness of the action.

Her ears flicked once then twice, and she lifted her nose up to catch the faint scent on the breeze. Her pupils widened to catch the limited light and increase her vision.

Prey.

Deer.

Could she retrieve a midnight snack?

Licking her muzzle, she pushed up and began to track breakfast. Paws were silent and confident as they strode across the landscape.

Unnoticed time ticked away as she tracked and stalked the deer. Crouching under natural camouflage to hide her white fur, the she-jaguar waited while she watched the deer munch on a patch of grass covered with dew droplets. The long tail flicked once then twice.

In a smooth movement of sheer muscle, power, and grace, Melinda leapt out from her cover and took off after the deer. She followed the deer's frantic movements and leaps. One sure paw reached out and caught the hind leg enough to destabilize the deer's sprint. It was enough of a movement to pounce and drive sharp canines deep around the neck. Landing the remainder of her weight on the deer, she dragged it down, gave a twist of her head, and snapped the vertebrae clean with a sharp *pop* noise.

When she heard the last dying breath, Melinda released her death grip and licked her muzzle. Looking around, her ears flicked to catch the unsettled noise of smaller animals within the forest disturbed by the sudden chase to death, but she smelt no jaguars. Though, she spied the perfect tree to enjoy a leisurely midnight snack. Taking another grip on the deer, she walked over to the tree, dragging the deer between her paws and underneath her belly. With a few powerful leaps, claws dug into the bark, she carried the meal into the tree and laid it across a pair of forked branches.

Stretched across the branches, Melinda sliced open the belly with a talon, dove into the meal, and bloodied her muzzle. With absolute relish and hunger, she filled her belly with rich deer meat, partaking in the tastier options of the inner organs before enjoying the thick muscle of a hind leg. Finishing most of the deer carcass, she dragged it down from the tree, dug a burial hole, and dropped the remainder into it. She crouched, defecating to warn others away before covering everything with dirt.

Satisfied, an inelegant burp escaped while she pounded away from the area and located a different tree. Settling down among the branches, she groomed paws, face, and the rest of her fur in the precise, delicate manner of felines.

With a long yawn after her grooming session, Melinda looked over the quiet valley. A drift of wind brought the faint scent of the guardian jaguars. She knew they performed their territorial perimeter walk through the valley. From this current perch, she could tell the mark was old but refreshed by the patrols. It had been at least a day since the last patrol hit the mark. Another yawn widened her mouth, complete with a soft roar that drifted into a purr. At this particular moment, she really didn't want to drop back down and sniff out the trail or deal with those pesky males. She decided to worry about it later as her tail dropped and flicked. Resting head on paws, Melinda drifted into a light catnap.

* * * *

In the months following the dramatic Fire Moon events of their first triad and Goddess-blessed mating of Raphael, Sebastian, and Hillary, and the fall of two High Alphas and the rise of a new High Alpha for their clan, Collin Thompson was pleased to find things were starting to settle down. At least he hoped they were looking to return to a semblance of normal. The new High Alpha Alexander Thurston, the former High Alpha's middle son, wasn't pleased with his father's ruling or dealing with certain aspects of the clan. Alex put him in charge of the guardians, the protectors, and the soldiers of the clan, and it was a high honor for one of his age to be raised to such a prestigious status.

Alex handed down the latest orders to clean out the scum properties, owners, and clientele leftover from his father's vicious and cruel reign from the main village. Collin left the work under the watchful eyes of his new seconds, Luca Constantin and Zacharias Stein, and their guardian teams. Meanwhile, Collin took advantage and left on one of the valley perimeter runs that went by Paisley. He needed the run in his powerful jaguar form through the dense forest and mountainous terrain.

The dreams were driving him crazy. Dreams of a pale-haired female knelt between him and Luca on a bed as they caressed and adored her. For the past six nights, each dream became even more sensual and even more vivid.

Luca. Luca. There is an interesting cat. What could these dreams mean? Are they my mates? Luca, could Luca be my mate, Collin thought while he paced himself along the outermost perimeter.

A newcomer to the clan, Luca arrived a week after the fire moon and Alex accepted the High Alpha position. A quiet and unassuming golden jaguar, he requested a position with the guardians. Within weeks of reorganizing the chaos leftover from the old High Alpha, Luca proved himself to be invaluable.

Only within the last few days did Collin find himself lingering longer in Raphael and Sebastian's pub with Luca, talking over drinks and snacks when they finished their rounds. Collin deliberately put himself and Luca on the same time, often on rounds together, so he could learn more about the other man. Yet, something else drew him to the man.

It was something much deeper and more sensual between men. He wanted with Luca what Raphael and Sebastian had before they met their mate, Hillary. He didn't know if Luca enjoyed men in his bed, and Collin found himself shy.

Those dreams made his feelings for the man even more certain. There was something fate-driven between them. Did Luca have the same dreams and the same feelings? Who was this woman kneeling between them and adoring them with her gaze?

With a shake of his head, Collin concentrated on the task at hand, glad he decided to go this route by himself instead of asking Luca to join him. He needed to separate himself from the other man before he stepped the wrong way.

When he reached the closest border the clan had with Paisley, Collin added his scent in the form of urine to the various territorial markers. He lifted his head and sniffed.

Female. Unknown. Odd, she came from the direction of Paisley.

Collin swung his head and padded to a natural opening in the forest and mountain for a cat his size to slip through unnoticed. He put his nose down and found the female's scent. It was strong and fresh. After a brush of his paws against leaves and debris, he spotted an almost-perfect paw print in the fresh dirt next to a rock.

A jaguar female. She's still in the area.

Interested in finding out who this female was and why she wasn't registered with the clan, Collin got down to the business of tracking her scent. It was faint, placed by an experienced cat, but he could still find traces of it in the air, rocks, and leaves.

Around a bend, he saw a tuft of white fur caught on a prickly bush. He trotted to it and sniffed. It was hers. He rubbed his cheek and chin over it, marking the fur with his scent to warn her how this was his territory and he was on her trail.

After another mile of tracking, impressed by her travels through the mountain, he caught sight of a disturbed area of ground by another tumble of boulders. He moved and pulled back his lips with a grimace, revealing his fangs.

A deer carcass with her excrement to warn others from taking her kill was buried. As an Alpha guardian, he growled and ignored her attempt to warn him. He moved around the burial site and deliberately added a harsh, fresh scent. Trotting to the nearby tree, he leapt and raked his claws down the bark.

Who is this female who dares to hunt within my clan's territory?

With a snarl at her arrogance, he returned to the trail. He leapt over a fallen log with a strong push of his paws. He then jumped to land on a boulder. Once there, he used it as an advantage point to look around for the female. His ears flicked, his nose twitched to catch her unique scent, and then he went down another path through the forest. He pushed off one boulder, bounded off a second one, hit the ground, and raced away.

He followed her trail to a large old tree and circled it a few times. Then he caught sight of claw marks in the trunk. Lifting his head, he reared and put his front paws on the trunk while he stared higher into the branches.

A lean cat stretched comfortably in the nook of three limbs. A long tail flicked and twitched while the cat continued its peaceful nap. From the size, he could tell this was the jaguar he'd tracked for the last few miles. Only, he didn't expect this unusual sight.

A moon-white jaguar. Can one of her kind truly exist? A daughter of our beloved Goddess Selene is here in my clan's valley.

Confused by the sight of her, Collin sat down and flicked his tail while he chuffed. He had heard of the gifted Luna jaguars as a myth, a childhood story. They were the daughters of Selene. The myth mentioned how they were given to clans as a token of her blessing. Along with other gifts, the Luna moon jaguar could even grow the fabled white moon flowers. He wondered if anyone within the clan knew more about the Lunas, for now he had one asleep in front of him.

It's time to wake, Luna beauty.

He climbed the tree and decided to be playful. He sniffed at the flicking tail and over to her lovely face. He lifted a paw and batted the tail a few times in play and query. He chuffed loudly and dug his claws into the bark to wait for her reaction.

Her ears flicked at his noise, and her tail moved a little harsher. He gave it another gentle whack with his paw, not using his claws. With the second hit, she opened a pair of turquoise eyes, outlined in jaguar gold, and moved her head from her limb pillow. A yawn escaped, and her mouth opened to reveal healthy canines, until she found him perched on the branches below her.

Her lean body rippled with tension as she moved from sleep to flight mode at the sight of him, a territorial Alpha male. He tilted his head and watched her muscles bunch and move under the thick ivory fur dotted with pale-gray rosettes and markings.

To give her a bit of room, he leapt to the nearest boulder, swishing his tail to entice her to join and play. He wanted to see what this pretty female had inside her. He chuffed and tossed his head to invite her for a run.

She didn't move from her lazy position, but he caught the subtle hints that she wanted to flee. Her head turned while her gaze considered the options in front of her. She moved her gaze back to him, rose to her paws, and climbed with elegant grace out of her perch. When she moved near, she flicked her tail along his face, bumped her head against his shoulder, and chuffed.

He pushed her back with his head in answer. He could almost see her smile as she leapt over him in an astounding move and raced away. Snarling with a playful attack, he pushed off and followed her movements.

The mutual race went for a few miles, and they darted between trees and over piles of boulders, leaping across dangerous crevasses. Collin surged onto a higher path and vaulted down, knocking her off her paws, and they rolled across a sweet bed of grass near a waterfall and pond.

She came to a rest on her side, panting, and he rose over her in the dominant position. He nuzzled her shoulder, neck, and face, and licked her cheek, tantalized by her scent and the chase. Soon, the almost smoky essence of her arousal hit him, and he knew she wanted him.

He let her roll into position underneath him, tail held out of the way, and he clamped his teeth on her scruff as non-shifter jaguars did in reality. Members of his clan often mated in this form during the moon events, but he never felt the need or desire to take another. Until now. Until he smelled and chased this Luna down. Now if only he could see her human form. Could she be the woman in his dreams?

Her feline cry of pleasure lifted through the forest as he entered her from behind, rough in the form of jaguars. Unlike their natural counterparts, shifted jaguars didn't have the baculum and backward-facing spines to stimulate the female to ovulate. They could only reproduce in their human forms. Still, it was pleasurable for both partners to engage in sex in this form, at least according to other toms.

He pumped his hips, taking her deep as he shifted his grip on her scruff. She snarled in pleasure and lifted her hips to engage him. Collin found himself pleased to last longer than the rumored nine seconds of natural jaguars, even if they did go over a hundred times a day during a mating cycle.

Snarling with his release and feeling it stimulate hers, he released her quick and jumped off her. She turned to take a swipe of him in typical female fashion and rose from their mating position to lie down near the pond.

Intrigued by this gorgeous Luna female, Collin returned to her side. He nuzzled her with his muzzle, licked her face to cleanse her, and lay behind her on his side. He dropped his head to his paws for a catnap.

Chapter 2

Refreshed after his catnap, Collin lifted his head with a powerful yawn. Back in human form, he stretched his legs and reached for the pretty lady he tracked and chased through the mountains. "So, darling, are you going to tell me…" he started to ask in a low voice, but his hand only found grass. When he realized the grass next to him was empty and cold, he opened his eyes and searched the immediate clearing. "Holy dark moon! I can't believe this is happening. Damn infuriating female," he cursed.

Collin rubbed the heels of his hands against his eyes as he rolled into a sitting position. He had a nasty feeling she would be nowhere near the waterfall. Once again, she left him behind to track her ass. Damn mysterious female and her secrets.

Damn, how the in the name of the Goddess can I lose her again? Alex is going to rip me a new one if he hears about this mistake. I wanted to see her human form to see if she's the one who haunts my dreams. Now I need to track her all over again. Blasted female. Who the hell is she?

Annoyed at the extra trouble the feline was giving him, he changed back into his jaguar form and rolled to his paws. After another stretch to ready his cat, he searched around the grassy area to confirm his thoughts. Then he leaped and rushed back up the boulders surrounding the waterfall. Used to her scent, he found the faint markers and trailed her elusive tail.

This time, she led him over the edge of the valley, the clan's highest perimeter, and down a forest-covered slope. Within a few minutes, he plopped his rump down at the border between forest and grass. The Paisley Animal Clinic and Shelter nestled alone at the end of the single road. There were lights upstairs and downstairs, along with the noises and scents of smaller animals. He had a feeling her trail would lead right to the building.

Gotcha, pretty Luna. Now all I need is a name and a human face to go with your cat. It shouldn't be too hard of a detail to locate.

Deciding to give her a few more minutes to see if her human version appeared, he settled his paws under his body and curled among the bushes to watch and wait.

* * * *

With her heart thumping wildly against her chest, scantily clad in only the thin silk robe she clutched to her body, Melinda shoved a hand through her tangled hair.

"Oh sweet moon and Goddess, what have I done?" she moaned as she slid down and crumpled on the floor.

She wouldn't get away from him, this powerful golden jaguar male. He would track her. He would be looking for her. Perhaps he followed her home and waited outside. Pulling her lower lip in to sink her teeth down, she turned one flushed cheek against the cool panel of the door.

Somehow she knew he would be outside, among the trees, crouched and watching the building with those intense eyes.

Why did she have sex in her jaguar form with an unknown Alpha male? She had never done such a crazy thing before. Though something about her jaguar brought out the sensuality inside her around other jaguars, she usually managed to keep her need under control. She could blame it on the dreams if his human form matched one of the males.

"It sure didn't happen this time, girl," she muttered.

Melinda wanted to crawl to the nearest window and peek out to look for those distinctive, reflective eyes peering back. She knew she shouldn't. It would encourage the male to come closer to her safe haven. Her one safety net until she heard from the High Alpha she could join as a temporary member and enter the valley to begin her internship with them until, hopefully, they would approve her as a full member.

Only now, one of those clan members, an Alpha guardian, now found out her deepest, darkest secret. She was one of the mythical white jaguars. A myth came true. She was a moon daughter of the Goddess Selene, who protected all jaguars.

Her previous High Alpha believed the old parts of the myth and wanted to capture and lock her in his mansion. He wanted to use her as a sex slave to empower him and a select few males, strengthened them by having sex with her. It was pure rape. She learned about their plans through the help of a guardian friend. With the assistance of her friend, she packed her things in a single night and escaped.

With her degrees and knowledge of both human and animal medicine, Melinda knew any clan would welcome her as a transfer. She didn't realize how hard it would be to get the transfer papers through to the High Alpha.

"Breathe, girl, breathe. Now isn't a time for a breakdown. It's time to get your ass moving. You're needed downstairs," she ordered herself. She pushed herself off the floor and couldn't stop herself from moving to the window. She flicked the blinds opened for a peek.

Iridescent pale-blue eyes, which reminded her of the ocean she left behind, glimmered with a bit of gold back from the tree line.

Holy sweet moon, he followed her home. He was there, watching her.

Melinda released the blinds, pressed her fingers to her face, and breathed in his scent. It was masculine, woodsy, and a little citrusy, and she could locate him again from the smell alone. She didn't want to shower away this essence.

Moving to the bedroom, she caught sight of her appearance in the dresser mirror. Her pale hair tangled from the rushed shift back and her fingers. Her eyes were dark from latent arousal. Her skin was rosy and flush with color.

Oh yeah, anyone would see she had done something naughty.

After she changed into fresh underwear and scrubs, she studied her mop of hair. With a little curl of her lips, she pulled it into a tight twist and secured it with a few pins. She grabbed some face powder and dusted her face in an attempt to hide evidence of the restless night. With a sigh, she slicked her lips with gloss and went to the living room. She picked up keys and the white jacket and slid her feet in her favorite Crocs.

She stepped outside, forced herself to not look to the woods, locked the door, and raced down the stairs. She went to the back door of the clinic and surrendered to curiosity. There was a brief flicker of a long spotted tail as it disappeared in the trees. The jaguar strolled away.

Damn, now he knows where I live, work, and what I look like as a human.

She pulled in her lower lip and chewed at the gloss.

The door opened from the inside.

"Hey, Doc, did you forget something?" one of the techs asked.

"No. No, thought I saw something in the woods. How is everyone doing this morning? All our furry friends pass a good evening?" she asked as she stepped into the clinic.

The tech nodded.

After she slid her arms into the white coat, she slipped the stethoscope around her neck and began her day.

* * * *

Intrigued as all hell by the mysteries surrounding the white jaguar since he found her home and work location, Collin watched the elegant lady walk down from the upper apartment, turn to meet his stare, and enter the clinic. From the distance, she was a rare beauty.

He wanted to know more, wanted to know everything about her, and, damn it, he wanted her name.

Holy sweet moon! It was the woman in his dreams. This was his mate!

He raced the entire perimeter check back to the clan's valley. He ran to his home, which was grouped together near other guardians at one end of the small town, and transformed in his backyard. Still unsettled from the mating and the female herself, Collin paced his yard.

"Sweet dark moon! Damn, Collin, is that you? Where the hell have you been?"

Spun around on the ball of his foot, Collin watched the tall, rangy form of Luca Constantin walk around the corner of his home. The second-generation son of immigrant Greeks, his Mediterranean heritage appeared within in his olive-toned skin and deep-brown hair. His reflective dark-green eyes held a worried look within their gaze when Collin met them. Luca stopped his movements when he saw Collin remained nude.

"Hey, Luca. What are you talking about? I was out on long patrol," Collin reminded him.

"No one is supposed to go alone, your orders to the others, remember?"

Collin shrugged. "Spur of the moment on my end. I didn't schedule it."

"Oh, so if something happened, no one would have any idea where you went."

Collin opened his mouth and then closed it when he realized Luca was correct. "Damn. I'm sorry. I didn't think."

"No, you didn't. Plus, you were gone longer than a normal patrol. What happened to you? Was it rogues?" Luca stepped closer and stopped short. He lifted his head and sniffed. "What in the moon…"

"Oh yeah…" Collin turned and sniffed himself. He caught her scent lingering on his skin and smiled. "Not a rogue, but an unexpected encounter on the road near Paisley. It's what held me up out there." Collin brushed past Luca to enter his home.

Luca grabbed him around his upper arm and yanked him to a stop. Leaning closer, he sniffed Collin's shoulder and neck deliberately to capture the intoxicating scent. His eyes darkened with arousal as he stepped against Collin's side.

"Luca, get a hold of yourself." Collin placed his hands on Luca's shoulders to push him back. "What got into you?"

Luca narrowed his eyes in a dark glare. "Who the hell is she? Who do I smell on you?"

Unsettled by Luca's strange reaction to the Luna's scent, Collin stared at the other man. "I met her on the patrol. She came from Paisley."

"She isn't from the clan."

"No, she isn't, but I'm pretty sure she wishes to become a member. She's definitely a jaguar."

Luca sneered. "Did she screw you as a way to get in?"

Collin yanked his arm from Luca's grasp. "Now that kind of jealous and snotty attitude pisses me off. You don't know anything about the situation or what happened between us out there to make that kind of call. What Goddess-given right do you have to question my behavior? You have no claim upon me."

"Though, I know you want to have a claim on me. Why else do you send me all those sensual dreams?" Luca murmured, moved until he cornered Collin against the glass door.

"Dreams? Have you been dreaming? What are your dreams about?"

"For days to the point where I can barely sleep. They're about you, damn dark moon—you and a female. When I'm awake, I've noticed the looks you give me. The scent you put off around me. You desire me."

"Perhaps it was foolish of me to even consider you," Collin snarled.

"No. No. I was… am new to the clan. My position is tenuous. To allow myself to fall for you, the leader and my captain of the guardians, it's crazy." Luca curled a hand against Collin's face. "I find myself wanting to be with you all time. The dreams only intensified the feelings. Then there is this female with us. Who is she?"

"You do? I…" Collin swallowed hard before he continued. "I thought you didn't care for another male."

"I'm picky when it comes to male lovers, but you…" Luca stepped back and shoved a hand through his hair. He shook his head and stared back at Collin. "From the moment I entered the clan and saw you. These blue eyes resemble the colors of a shifting sea. You intrigued me with your grace, your power, your kindness toward everyone within the clan, and your welcoming nature to the newcomers. I wanted to know more, but I didn't wish to push my luck. I didn't want to run the risk of being tossed out and thrown back to my old clan. Then the dreams started to come to me, and I knew fate was helping."

"Were members of your clan cruel?"

"Some members were, depending on the situation, while others were downright vicious. You know how clans can become separated. Some cats create small cliques within a clan to torment others or push their ideas and suggestions. If the High Alpha or other guardians don't step in and squash them, the cliques can become the quiet rulers and power." Luca stared at the ground.

"This is what happened in your home clan?"

"It was only a matter of time before a coup happened. I and others spoke about leaving before it went down. I got a text from a fellow guardian two nights ago. The clique took over, and many were either killed or imprisoned. They were ruthless. Many needlessly lost their lives."

"Unbelievable how shit like that can happen."

"Others wanted to find a way to report it, but no idea how to contact the governing council, if there is even one, over all the High Alphas. There is no one to protect those under the ruthless leaders." Luca shook his head. "It's criminal."

"Perhaps it's something to speak about with Alex."

"He's one High Alpha, one voice among many."

"It's a start to a possible solution."

"Maybe. About this delicious scent…" Luca stepped closer and sniffed Collin's neck once more. "Who is she?"

"I don't know. We were, umm…" Collin flushed. "We were in jaguar form. Only."

Luca lifted an eyebrow. "You mated in jaguar form?"

"Yeah. We mated once and took a nap. We were in the clearing by the small waterfall, not far from the Paisley border road. It was the first time I took a female as a jaguar."

"Interesting. Usually mated couples have sex in their cat forms during full-moon runs, not singles. She was interested in you, or there was something else. Did you see her other form?"

"From a distance after I tracked her home to a clinic in Paisley. She lives right on the edge of the town, close to the valley. She disappeared while I slept and made me follow her scent."

Luca snorted and shook his head.

"Yeah, yeah. Some guardian captain I am to let a female sneak away. I know."

"A gorgeous female can do it to anyone."

"There is something else."

"You mean something other than mating as jaguars? I say this is a pretty darn big deal. What else could there be?" Luca trailed a finger over Collin's broad shoulder.

"She's a Luna jaguar."

Luca stopped and stared. "Luna? Is she completely white with gray markings?"

"Just like it's spoken in the stories. I thought I was imagining her when I saw her asleep in the tree. Could one exist, or could she be an albino?"

"What color were her eyes?"

"They were a turquoise color with the gold rims."

"Then she's not albino. They're always a red or pink. She's a true Luna. We would know for sure when she shifts and she has a crescent moon birthmark. It would explain your sensual pull since a Luna exudes sexuality in cat form."

"Oh...And you?"

"Her scent is all over you, though I'm still attracted to you for you." Luca glanced to the side to a particular plant growing next to the door. "It isn't because of the stupid catnip growing over there. Why the hell do you have it growing there?"

"I um...like to eat it like any other cat." Collin felt a flush rising. "It makes a wonderful tea when dried and mixed with other flowers and herbs."

"Though it drives some of us nuts or makes others stoned."

"There is the possibility of it happening to some."

Luca reached out and pinched out a small branch. He rolled and broke the leaves between his fingers to release the intoxicating scent between them. Both moaned and growled, their bodies reacting to the nip.

"Must have you," Luca grumbled in Collin's ear when he pressed the naked man against the cold window of the patio door.

"Inside. I have stuff inside," Collin said, groaning when Luca rolled his hips and nudged his arousal against him. He managed to reach behind him, fumble for the handle, and yank the door to the side.

They nearly toppled into the living room when the door opened. Only their quick catlike reflexes saved them. Luca grumbled and pushed Collin further into the room until they found the sofa.

"Got something here?" Luca looked around the relatively well-kept and styled room.

"I left something in the box on the side table. The one with the old-fashioned map print," Collin said, waving a hand to the far table.

"Who did you have last in here?" Luca demanded.

Collin shook his head. "No one since I met you. I put it there with hope of something."

"Something?"

Collin nodded.

"Looks like this is the something we both wanted."

"Yeah, I think this is what I imagined."

"Then you better go lie down and get it," Luca said as he stepped back and began to shed his clothes.

"So bossy and aggressive, I like. Are you going to tie me up?" Collin said with a low purr.

"I will if you don't behave and do what I tell you," Luca threatened with a show of sharp teeth.

With a husky laugh, Collin dropped back on the sofa, threw his hands behind, and searched for the box. He managed to open the latch, flip the top back, and find the bottle of lube he stashed there in case he ever found himself lucky with Luca. It was the truth when he told Luca there was no one who had crossed his radar since they met. When he brought the lube in front of him, he double-checked the expiration date.

"Still good?" Luca raised an eyebrow.

"Caught my check, didn't you?"

"It's been a while for me, too." Luca moved toward Collin and the sofa and knelt on the edge.

"I'm surprised. The darn thing isn't expired. We're good," Collin said as he waved the bottle.

"Good. Keep it handy," Luca said before he bent over and captured Collin's lips in a heated kiss.

Once again the passion flared between them. While Luca kissed the length of Collin's neck, he slid his right hand down to Collin's crotch. He cupped him and gave his sac a little extra squeeze.

Collin felt his cock jerk and twitch in Luca's hand. His balls pulled up, and he was afraid he was going to explode before they did anything. He moaned when Luca wrapped his fingers around his rigid cock and began to pump with short, sharp strokes from his base to his sensitive knob. There Luca rubbed the head, constricted under the rim, one finger glancing over the glans. Then Luca went back to the quick pumps.

"Oh hell…" Collin leaned his head back against the sofa's arm. He tried to suck in air to control his body under the heady touch.

"I want to watch you come," Luca said as he continued the heat and friction with those tugs and jerks.

"No…Not without you," Collin said with a moan and a shake of his head.

His moan was muffled when Luca's warm lips came down on his mouth. Their tongues tangled around one another as Luca plunged his passionately into Collin while he kept his hand moving over Collin's cock. Luca teased and tormented him.

Collin's mouth mimicked everything Luca did, from the sensual dance of their tongues, to a nip on Luca's bottom lip with his teeth.

The slapping sound of flesh-on-flesh filled the room as Luca pumped his cock with ever-increasing speed. Grunts fell from Collin's lips when Luca leaned back as they both dragged air into their lungs.

Collin closed his eyes, and his cock splattered a shot of cum all over Luca's hand and their bellies. His hips lifted and moved under Luca's touch. He shuddered with a moan as Luca continued to pump him until he was emptied. His body twitched with a few more post-orgasm shudders. His cock was still hard and ready for more action.

He heard the snick of a cap opening before he felt fingers and cold lube brushed against his puckered opening. He twisted his head to one side as his fingers dug into the cushions, and he moaned as Luca worked fingers into him. Luca increased the steady pressure in and around his rectum, and it sent sensations flying through the rest of his body.

Luca sank another finger down to his knuckle, twisted, and flexed before he thrust in and out. He nudged against the sensitive gland which had Collin moaning and twisting on the sofa. He lifted one of Collin's legs to the back of the sofa and the other around his hips as he moved forward. Placing the broad head against the well-lubricated opening, Luca slid his thick shaft all the way to the root in one thrust.

Collin gasped at the sensation, his legs twitched around Luca, and even his toes began to curl. The erotic feeling of the exquisite fullness drove away any bit of pain from the hard, quick entry. As he learned to breathe and relax, he dragged his gaze up Luca's body and met his stare. It was full of need, lust, and something far deeper.

"Dark moon, you're tight. So tight and hot, you feel so good. Are you okay? Can I move?" Luca asked.

The driving beat of his heart filled his ears, and he almost didn't hear Luca's soft words. Collin managed to nod and lift his hips to encourage Luca.

In full control, Luca withdrew until only the cock head remained inside and teased the opening. He pumped shallow a few times, in and out, stretching the ring before he sank deep inside with a forceful stroke. With gradual surges, Luca increased the pressure, speed, and depth of his strokes. As the escalation continued, they moaned together. Luca braced his hands on either side of Collin's head on the sofa arm. With the support, he slammed his hard cock harder and deeper into Collin's tight channel. The sound of flesh slapping on flesh filled the room once more.

Collin's jaw tightened as Luca filled him, surged into him, and hit his prostate with every deep stroke. The brush of Luca's soft pubic hair hitting his cock and balls caused more sensitivity.

Luca took them on a rough, hard ride, which went right to the edge, but he backed off at the last moment. Collin gritted his teeth and groaned at being held back. He sank his fingers into Luca's ass.

When he was ready to blow, his cock so loaded it would explode at any moment, Collin met Luca's gaze. "Please...Luca."

Luca lowered a hand to Collin's cock. He began to pump in time with his deep strokes, his fingers pressing against the ropey veins, and he brushed along the rim of the deep plum head. "Are you gonna come?"

"Hell, yes, let me. Damn you to the moon."

Luca smiled in a wicked, wanton way. He gave Collin a final twist, which had him exploding with a loud cry. Neither one cared about the ropes of cum that splashed down Luca's hand and spread across Collin's belly. Collin's violent eruption caused his channel to clench and clamp around Luca's thick cock. Luca tumbled over the edge with a final hard shove and sent his cum deep inside Collin.

The final ride into oblivion was hard and hot and something neither one had experienced before.

After coming down and still trying to find his breath, Luca managed to pull out of Collin's tender opening. He twisted and dropped on the sofa behind. He wrapped an arm around Collin to pull him against him.

"Holy dark moon, what was that?" Collin whispered as he came back into himself.

"The loving of mates," Luca murmured in Collin's ears.

"I'll take more of that," Collin said and repeated it in a soft voice as sleep began to claim him.

"Same here."

Together, they drifted into the sleep of the sated and oblivious.

Chapter 3

Over the course of the next couple of days, in between their patrols and passionate overheated moments of sex, Collin and Luca were called into Alex's office together. Until the main High Alpha office was refinished in the central building within town, and the cleaning process of the unwanted businesses and their clientele removed, Alex set his temporary office on the first floor of his father's large three-story mansion.

The state of the High Alpha office was a disorganized disaster. Alex was under the water immediately, tugged by complaints and unable to figure out the finances. With Collin's help and recruitment, twin males, Benjamin and Samuel, were brought in early and reorganized everything. The organizer, Benjamin, took over the entire front office with quick, brutal efficiency and pulled a lot of stress and strain off Alex's shoulders and the financial whiz kid, Sam, changed all the files, accounts, and books into computerized accounting records. Within a few hours, he soon reported to Alex how his father double-dipped into multiple accounts and hid hundreds of thousands of dollars from the clan. Alex asked Sam to continue finding more accounts. Almost every day to everyone's surprise, Sam uncovered more hidden money as he went deeper through the records.

"Good morning, guardians," Ben said as he glanced up from his desk and computer and nodded with respect to them. "How are you both doing today?"

"We're well, Ben. How goes everything with you?" Collin asked the young jaguar. "How's the boss man?"

"Still a little on the stressed end with the cleanup and rebuilding. His father did jack shit for the clan, and there's a lot we need to do. Luckily, Sam is finding the money to provide the funds."

"He found more?"

Ben nodded. "Three more accounts in Switzerland."

"Holy dark moon!"

"I think the knowledge of his father hiding all this money eats more at him than some of the physical things he did."

"There's nothing he could've done except take over the clan."

"Which saved everyone," Ben added.

"Now we need to save him," Luca said in a low tone.

"Exactly," Collin said, pressing a hand on Luca's arm. "Ben, Alex called and wanted to see us. Is he available?"

"Let me check," Ben said and hit the button on the intercom. "Alpha Alex, guardians Collin and Luca are here."

"Send them in," Alex replied over the intercom.

Ben waved them to the door.

"Thanks, Ben," Collin said.

"Could I get you something to drink before you go?"

Collin glanced to Luca, who shook his head. "No, we're good."

Ben nodded and returned to his work as the two men opened one of the double doors into the larger office.

At the far end, behind a beautiful walnut desk, a potent, powerful Alpha male jaguar sat in a comfortable chair. A top-of-the-line laptop sat on one side, paperwork scattered across another end, and a stack of folders and binders were gathered in various piles on the credenza and a bookcase. He shoved a hand through reddish-brown hair that flopped over a high forehead, and tilted his head to one side until the other males heard the crack of some vertebrae pop into place.

"That sounded like it felt good, Alpha," Collin teased his friend and High Alpha as they stopped in front of the desk.

Alexander Thurston looked up from his work, dropped the pen from his right hand, and smiled at getting caught. "I need to have my entire back cracked after sitting in this chair for so long." He rose gracefully to his six-four height and bumped knuckles with Collin, but shook hands with Luca. He then waved them to sit in the comfortable chairs placed in front of the desk. "Sit, please. How are you two doing?"

"Good. Patrols are clear. Rogues are quiet for now. Only one small hitch, but I'm taking care of it with Luca," Collin said.

"A hitch?" Alex sat down and leaned back in the chair.

"Found the tracks and scent of an unknown female jaguar near the path down to Paisley when I did the long patrol a few days ago. She's not one of ours. Do you have record of a female wanting to join the clan in the last few weeks or months?" Collin leaned forward, bracing his elbows on his thighs.

"I'm not sure. I put all requests aside for the time being. I'm still trying to take care of our own and getting our clan straightened out has been a full-time task and taken most of my time," Alex said.

"This one would be kind of important, boss." Collin glanced at Luca, who nodded.

Alex looked between them. "Why? What's going on with her?"

"We think she's a Luna...or...at least, I think she's a Luna. I saw her...mated with her as jaguars, sir, in a clearing near the old waterfall..." Collin cleared his throat and blushed.

"Then he returned and mated with me," Luca finished.

Alex lifted an eyebrow. "Do the two of you believe you are a triad with this unknown female? A Luna female? I heard about these rare white females. A blessing for the clan who has this gift from the Goddess, but I've never met one myself."

The two guardians glanced at one another and nodded. Their hands reached for each other, clasped and fingers entwined.

"We've been having dreams of each other and a pale-haired female for weeks now. It's a sign of mates," Collin said.

"Dreams? Both of you are having dreams?"

"Yes, we are."

"Another triad." Alex sat back.

"I believe the Goddess has given us this gift," Collin replied. "Only we need to find her and speak with her."

"You need to find her? You haven't spoken with her? As a human?"

Collin shook his head. "She got away from me."

"How did you let her get away?"

"We mated and napped as cats. When I woke, she was gone." Collin shrugged a shoulder. "Shit happens. I followed her again to her home and work. I need help to identify her so Luca and I can speak with her."

"Okay then, as you said, we need to know who she is," Alex agreed and hit the intercom. "Ben."

"Yes, sir."

"Where is the folder of transfers?"

"It's not a folder now. The numbers grew since you took over," Ben said.

"Fine. Where are they?"

"I put everything in the blue binder marked *Transfer* on the credenza behind you, sir. They are organized by sex and then by last name," his efficient assistant replied.

"Right. Of course you did. Thank you, Ben." Alex grimaced, cleared his throat, and turned the chair around. As Ben stated, he found the binder right where his assistant said it was located. He lifted it onto his desk and opened it.

The guardians tried not to chuckle at their Alpha's predicament.

"Yeah. Yeah, don't give me shit. I can handle a pair of smart-ass kits. I have enough on my plate to deal with to bother with them," Alex said, hearing them clearing their throats and muffling their snickers.

"Sorry, boss," Collin said.

"What do you know about your lady?" Alex asked as he flipped pages to reach the female section and looked at them.

"Umm. Turquoise eyes. A possible Luna. She lives above and works at the Paisley Animal Clinic either as the vet or one of the techs," Collin listed.

Alex blinked slowly and waited.

Collin grinned.

"That's it?"

"Yeah. I tracked her to the clinic and caught a glimpse of her running down the stairs, but I couldn't see much of her human form."

Alex looked to Luca. "Anything?"

Luca shook his head. "I smelled her on him."

"Okay. This is going to make things a little difficult. We have twelve female candidates."

"Anyone list work as a vet as a background?" Collin suggested.

Sighing, Alex flipped through the pages, yanked a pad of small Post-it notes close, and used them to mark the possible candidates. "We're down to five."

"I had to fill in my coloring—eyes, hair, and all that," Luca said.

"She had turquoise or blue-green eyes. She had pale-gold hair, which matched the white coat," Collin offered.

"Hmm." Alex pulled the five possible ladies from the binder. He looked at the physical descriptions of each. "We're down to two ladies. One is a Doctor Melinda Hurst from the Vernal Moon Clan, who works for the clinic as another veterinarian, and the other is Paige Harrison, from the Venus Moon Clan, who is a vet tech for the local SPCA."

"Well, then I'm pretty sure she's the vet at the clinic, because she lived above it and carried a white coat of a doctor. So it must be Melinda…" Collin looked to Alex.

"Melinda Hurst," Alex said.

"Melinda Hurst," Collin repeated. "Beautiful name. We should return to the clinic and try to, umm…sniff the lady in question. We need to make sure she's the lady in our dreams." Collin grinned at Luca.

"Oh yeah, what a good plan. Walk up to a lady and sniff her ass. Real smart way to get your butt kicked, Collin," Luca said with a roll of his eyes.

"Best we got."

"We'll look like idiots," Luca said.

Collin shrugged.

"Sir. Heads up! Incoming female!" Ben warned over the intercom as the door swung in hard.

"Alex, we need to talk before I knock these two boneheads senseless and nutless. Hi, Collin, Luca. I'm sorry, but I'm going crazy here," Hillary Haywood-Salazar said, storming into the office. Her petite, pear-shaped body had a noticeable swell around her belly. She was filled with vibrant energy as she slammed hands on full hips. Her towering guardian mates, one golden and one dark, followed right on her heels.

"Hillary *querida*, you shouldn't break into the High Alpha's office like this, not without an appointment. *Perdone*, Alpha," Raphael Salazar, the dark-haired guardian, pleaded in his Latino-accented voice.

Hillary whipped a dark look over her shoulder at one of her two mates.

"It's all right, Raphael. Hillary, how wonderful to see you," Alex said as he rose from his chair and moved around his desk. He opened his arms and embraced the smaller female in a light hug, cautious of her swollen belly. He ignored the light growls from the mated guardian toms with a warm chuckle.

"Oh, ignore them since they're being extra grumbly lately," she said, smacking the golden one, called Sebastian, in the stomach with the back of her hand.

"Ow! It was him, not me," Sebastian Haywood said, rubbing his flat, muscular abdomen, and he gave her a playful pout.

"*Gracias, mi amor*," Raphael said in a low tone.

"It's both of you, so don't even go there," Hillary snapped.

"Okay. Okay. What is going on with you three?" Alex said, using his alpha tone to break off another argument.

"They knocked me up and now think I'm fragile," Hillary said, crossing arms under her breasts after a stroke against the upper swell of her belly. She shifted her shoulders back and forth.

"It's not that, *querida*..." Raphael started.

"No, we don't think..." Sebastian started at the same time.

"Ha! Exactly. You don't think." Hillary lifted a hand to stop both of them in their tracks. "They're driving me up a frigging wall, Alex. You would think I'm the first female to get pregnant."

"You're our lady to get pregnant with our cubs. It's a first for us," Sebastian said.

Hillary rolled her eyes. "Alex, please? I have two and half months more of this pregnancy, and I can't stand them much longer. I need a doctor, not those ancient midwives the other females trust. We have a clinic, a small hospital, standing empty for almost two years now. Isn't it time for a change, fill the clinic?"

"Okay. I agree with you. There needs to be a change of plans." Alex rubbed a hand over the back of his neck. "It seems we need to concentrate on the clinic and finding a general doctor, ob-gyn, pediatrician, and a surgeon, along with nurses."

"I think it would be most feasible. The sooner the better," Hillary grumped.

"What about our vet?" Collin asked. "They have to go through med school."

"Our vet? What do you mean..." Sebastian asked as he walked further in and nudged Raphael's shoulder. He looked at Collin and then Luca. "Whoa...You and...Nice, good for you two."

"Bastian, now isn't the best time," Raphael said.

Collin blushed and rose from the chair. "Yeah, well, we were a little unexpected but..." Collin dropped a hand on Luca's shoulder.

Luca glanced up from his position in the chair and smiled in quiet support.

"Not now. She would be a good possibility." Alex continued to rub his neck. "Okay. Collin, Luca, I need to put you two in charge of going to the clinic, opening it, and taking inventory of the inside. See what we need and then start ordering. Stop off and see Sam before you leave for the clinic account and card. I believe he set one in place for such an emergency." He glanced to Hillary. "About how long do we have?"

"Another clueless tom," Hillary muttered, covering her face with her hand.

"Sorry. Only had brothers and my mother didn't stick around," Alex said with a pleading look of forgiveness.

"Another two or maybe two and a half months, which is an estimate without a doctor's knowledge, and I believe I'm carrying more than one, so things are more difficult to estimate. Our gestation is four and a half to five months, High Alpha and it is a period set halfway between a human and jaguar pregnancy," she explained.

"Right. Understand," Alex said and rubbed his hands together. "We have about two months to get things set in place before the cubs come."

"But I would request before then for check-ups, along with all the other females who are expecting, those who gave birth, and newborn cubs who need a doctor who understands both human and jaguar physiques." She pressed a hand to her swollen belly in the quintessential touch all pregnant females seem to do when they're expecting.

"Don't worry about this. I will find a doctor to care for you and all the others. This is my position to care for those in my clan. You need to care for yourself, your cubs, and yes, even your annoying, possessive, aggravating mates," Alex said.

"Hey," Sebastian said.

Alex looked over Hillary's shoulder with a lifted eyebrow. "Suck it up, tomcat."

Hillary chuckled, turned, and wrapped her arms around Sebastian's chest. She tugged hold of Raphael's wrist and yanked him against her back. She sighed when his arms enclosed around the both of them. Both males curled a hand around either side of her belly, in both a protective and comforting fashion of the growing cubs.

The others smiled at the loving triad.

"Go on home, you three. We'll figure out the clinic and doctor issue. I promise," Alex said.

"Thanks, Alex. Sorry about the intrusion," Hillary murmured from within her mates' arms. She leaned against her mates as they left the office.

After the triad left, Alex returned to his desk, opened a drawer, and pulled out a key ring. He tossed it to Collin, who snagged it out of the air with an easy catch. "Those will open the clinic. I had the locks changed out and all the windows changed to impenetrable glass at the same time we did the guardian and jail buildings and the new High Alpha building. It has Wi-Fi installed, and the utilities should be working fine. Check with Sam on all the details."

"You got it, boss. I know what to do," Collin said as he nodded to Luca, who rose without a word.

"Good. Let's get this job done. The sooner the better if at all possible, otherwise we'll have a bunch of females on our tails. If you can find your lady at the same time, it will be even better," Alex said. "Keep me updated about your progress with both projects."

Collin nodded as the two guardians left the office. He turned past Ben's desk and went down the hallway to his twin brother's office. "We need to see Sam," he informed Ben.

"No problem. Twin is there," Ben said.

"Good. Thanks," Collin said with a wave.

Ben waved back and went to work. He nodded to Luca, who nodded back.

Collin took hold of Luca's hand and half dragged him down the hallway. He knocked on Sam's door and poked his head around the door. "Hey, Sam, can Luca and I bug you for a few minutes?"

An identical copy of Benjamin looked up from the desk filled with multiple monitors and even more paperwork and files. His smile was a little shyer than his brother's, but Samuel nodded and waved them inside. "What can I do for you, Collin, Luca?"

Collin walked in and leaned a hip against the corner of Sam's desk. "Alex sent us in on a mission. We need to fix and stock the clinic, along with finding doctors, nurses, and staff. A certain female is kicking our asses to get moving. Alex mentioned you would have the funds."

"Ahh, yes, the clinic. I went through the various floors of the clinic myself. The previous doctor used the first floor and left alone the upper ones. The stupid idiot didn't bother to care for anyone in our clan. I'm amazed more of us didn't die under his care," Sam said.

"So we have a bigger mess on our hands than we first thought."

"Yes, I'm afraid to say. I made a tentative list of possible equipment and supplies. On Alex's agreement, I had the flooring replaced, the walls repainted, and all the lighting redone. Also, all the previous flooring, cabinetry, desks, and other framework were replaced where needed. I went ahead and ordered all new gurneys and wheelchairs since the others were ruined by looters," Sam said while digging through the files, and he unearthed a thick one and held it out Collin.

"You did all this?"

"Hmm. It needed all of it and more. There's been no doctor for over two years, and looters got into the clinic more than once. I think they were after medicines, not that any were left. I also ordered new locking cabinets for medications, which we can't purchase without a doctor's authority."

"Understood. We'll do what we can until we find a doctor."

"Credit card is attached to the folder. Use it for any purchases concerning the clinic and keep the receipts," Sam said, reaching out with a pen and tapping the folder.

Collin opened it, and sure enough he saw a black credit card attached to it. He whistled low, knowing this was one of the high-premium ones.

"Alex wanted the best for the clinic, so it's what I managed to get from the bank after sorting out all of the various hidden accounts and sending them back to new ones in Paisley. I'll call the bank and put both of you as cosigners on the card until we have designated office staff in the clinic."

"Thanks, Sam. Is there anything else?"

Sam shook his head.

"Next stop is the clinic then," Luca said, breaking his silence.

"Guess so," Collin said as he waved to Sam.

They left the office and went past Ben, who waved again as they walked out. Since the clinic was in the middle of the clan's town, they decided to drive there, and climbed into Luca's golden-bronze Ford F-150 XLT.

Collin smoothed a hand over the adobe-cloth seats as he looked around the truck with a little bit of envy. "I do like this truck."

Luca grunted as he drove away from the Alpha's house and down to the valley's town center. "It became my getaway vehicle."

"What do you mean by that? When did you get this?"

"I chose it last year when I was with my old clan. I paid it off outright so I wouldn't have the debt on my shoulders and secretly sold my home to one of the other guardians."

"You were already planning on leaving?"

"Yeah, couldn't handle the crap the High Alpha was dealing, so I put in my request of transfer to the High Alpha here. Of course I didn't get the official approval until Alex took over, but I was allowed to move down and take a temporary position. I tossed all my stuff in the back and didn't look behind me when I took off."

"What about your family?"

"No one is left. My parents died during one of the many clashes between clans and rogues when I was younger," Luca said.

"Shit…I'm sorry, I didn't know." Collin reached out and gripped Luca's hand on the console. No wonder the golden jaguar kept quiet whenever they were together as a group of guardians at the club, having drinks, joking, or playing around.

"You didn't ask, nor do I volunteer the information easily."

"Are you an only cub?"

Luca shook his head. "I'm the youngest of triplets. My brothers are in different clans, with one in Montana, and the other is down in Texas. Both were forced out by the High Alpha when they showed too many Alpha qualities. In reality, he didn't want his favorite guardians being overthrown and someone else taking charge and finding out about his shady dealings. My brothers and some of their friends would have created a coup, but they didn't get the opportunity. They were broken apart before a plan of action was finalized." Luca's hand fisted against the wheel. "They barely made it out with their lives. I was kept out of it."

Silent, Collin moved his hand over Luca's thigh to calm him. He watched as color returned to the whitened knuckles and the fingers relaxed.

"Thanks." Luca cleared his throat. "We have twin younger sisters, and they're both in California clans with their respective mates and cubs. The girls scattered after our parents' death. I was the last to leave our home clan, going against hope things would change, but nothing did." He glanced at Collin when they stopped at one of four stoplights. He noticed Collin's strange stare. "What is it?"

"It's the longest I heard you talk about yourself or anything at all. I'm enjoying myself. I'm sitting back and listening to you. I don't want you to stop."

Luca snorted again. "Cut it out."

Collin chuckled.

"What about you?"

"What about me?"

Luca lifted an eyebrow. "Family? What about your family?"

"Oh, my family seems normal compared to yours. Do you want to hear it?"

"After my mess, yes, it'll be good to hear about a normal jaguar family."

"I'm a quadruplet cub with four older brothers. I'm the youngest, like you. We have triplet younger siblings. They're two sisters and a brother. My older brothers are guardians in nearby clans. The younger ones are still part of the Fire Moon Clan. My brother, Hadrian, is a younger guardian," Collin answered.

"Good-sized family. Are your parents still here?"

"Yeah. They're both still here, pleased to have Alex in charge after all the years under Irvine's rigid, ruthless control. My father is proud as a peacock when I told him about my promotion. He's been strutting about, his chest all puffed up when he's with his cronies, some of the elder guardians." Collin shook his head with a chuckle. "I should take you over to meet them."

"Not yet. Not until we find her."

"What? Why? I don't think my parents would give a shit if I'm in a gay relationship or with a female. Since the triad relationship happened, they understand things are changing in the clan. Unlike others, my father is proud of changes and is a forward thinker. He mentioned how my uncle is in a long-term gay relationship with another guardian multiple times. I think he's trying to hint at something."

"No, please, Collin, I'm not ready to meet family. We only found each other and our way. Our relationship is brand-new. Now we need to find her and deal with this clinic." Luca shoved a hard hand through his hair and growled.

Collin held up his hands. "Okay. Okay. I understand. I'm not going to push."

"Thank you for understanding."

"It's what I'm here for, to help and be with you."

Putting his hand back on the wheel, Luca turned the truck into parking lot in front of the multistoried clinic. He turned off the engine and got out.

"Hmm. Dark and silent now, what a waste. Like so much extra in this valley, we wasted so many resources vital to our survival," Collin muttered as he grabbed the folder, got out, and followed Luca to the front doors. He tugged the keys from his pocket and found the one to open the lock.

Together they walked in, Luca flipped on the lights, and both moved apart to begin searching and studying the clinic. As Sam mentioned, there was nothing left behind upstairs, so they returned to the main disaster of the first floor. Against the decay, they could find the repairs and replacements Sam spoke about, which were obvious against what was left behind, gathered in piles of debris. Luca kicked one pile and sneezed when dust drifted toward him.

"What a loss of a perfectly good space, and such a mess," Collin said. "Bless you."

Luca nodded and rubbed his nose after another harsh sneeze.

"Let's go check this floor out and see what we have here," Collin said.

After another rub of his nose and sniffle, Luca nodded.

"Are you allergic to dust?"

"It doesn't agree with my nose," Luca said.

Collin laughed, looped an arm around Luca's waist, and drew him deeper into the clinic.

Chapter 4

"Hello? Hello! Please tell me a doctor returned to us! Help! We need help!" a frantic call echoed through the clinic and got Collin and Luca racing back toward the front entrance.

"Holy sweet Goddess, Zacharias! Nathan, what the hell happened to him?" Collin demanded when he recognized the huge golden jaguar by the unusual ringlet formation around the left ear. He stared at the three large guardians who struggled to carry in the wounded guardian.

"I'm not sure, but he's not the only one injured, Collin, sir," Nathan Thomas, a younger guardian, said.

Another trio carried in a second jaguar and this one was black and a little smaller, but also wounded and unconscious.

"Who..." Collin asked since it was a little harder to identify patterns in the black fur.

"It's Grant Carson. He ran with Zacharias on the long patrol over by the border with the damn splinter group under Robert Thurston's control. What little we can tell, they were ambushed and attacked. I sent Austin, Hunter, and Wyatt out in one of the trucks when they were overdue, and they found them like this," Nathan said.

"Damn the dark moon! I knew things were too quiet along the border," Collin said, cursing himself.

Luca raced into the clinic and rushed back with two gurneys. Collin found himself thankful Sam ordered at least this little bit. He and Luca helped the others transfer the injured jaguars to the beds.

Collin growled under his breath about the splinter group and the Alpha who was almost as demented as his brother, the former High Alpha Irvine Thurston. "How long have they been like this?"

"I don't know. They show no signs of changing back to human form, which is strange. We always return to human form when unconscious or injured. We need a doc here bad, Collin. Their wounds are severe, smell nasty, and appear infected. I'm trained as a medic, but not a full-blown doctor. I would have no idea where to start treating them."

"It will be okay, Nathan. You did the right thing by bringing them home and to the clinic. We'll figure out something," Collin said, laying a hand on Nathan's shoulder.

Nathan nodded.

"What about the clinic you saw near Paisley? You can find the number and call it," Luca suggested.

Collin looked over the injured jaguars. "The clan…"

"You said most of Paisley knows about us. It doesn't matter now. We have lives on the line," Luca said.

"It's Zacharias and Grant lying there. There is no way we can leave them to deal with this on their own. We have no idea what they were hit with," Nathan added. He dropped a hand on his friends' shoulders.

The wounded golden feline was a favorite among most of the guardians. One of the older jaguars, he was friendly and outgoing, and taught most of them how to be a true guardian. The black cat was a younger member, but staunch and steady, always there when needed.

"Call Alex at the office, Nathan, and explain what happened and who I'm calling. You can give him a better idea of what happened with the others. We'll deal with the consequences after our clan members are healed." With a deep breath to steady himself before what he was about to do to open things further between the clan and outside world, Collin walked off and pulled out his cell phone. After a moment with local information, he dialed the number for the Paisley Animal Clinic.

"Looks like we don't have to go and sniff out her. She'll come to us," Luca said and called others in the clan to bring clean sheets, towels, bandages, and whatever else they could to the clinic.

"Let's hope and keep our fingers crossed that she's the one being sent," Collin called before the connection went through. "This is Collin Thompson from the Fire Valley. We're in desperate need of a doctor."

* * * *

Within moments, a dark-blue Ford Transit van with the Paisley Animal Clinic logo painted across it in multiple places rambled down the long road into town. In an expert motion, the van turned and backed into the parking lot of the clinic. Inside, Melinda flexed her fingers and gripped the steering wheel as she stared across the rest of the jaguar town settled in the bottom of the valley. It had been a place she had tried to enter since her arrival in Paisley and now she got the call to assist the local clan. As soon as the call came in to the clinic, she knew she was the only one to take the emergency, and she raced out to the prepared van. She had trained for both animals and humans throughout her long life.

Unable to wait, knowing lives were on the lines, she turned off the engine. The front door opened, and she hopped out. Another look around revealed no one walked around to her side. They waited for her to come to them. It was typical for clan behavior, when it came to outsiders, to scent first before asking questions and introductions. She reached back inside and yanked out the white coat. She tugged it on over the light-blue scrubs she had changed into after an earlier series of surgeries had messed up the first set. The last thing she grabbed was a large black bag. She slammed the door, walked around to the back, opened the back doors, and faced the clinic.

Two powerful males stood in front of the glass doors with Fire Valley Clinic silk-screened and etched across them. For some odd reason, the pair reminded her of the men in her dreams.

No, now isn't the time for me to go there. I have work to do here.

Melinda stopped and returned their stares with calm and grace, not backing down. "Did one of you call for help? I'm Doctor Melinda Hurst from the clinic."

The men looked at each other in an odd fashion and then back to her.

"Melinda Hurst?" one repeated her name and stepped closer.

She nodded. "Yes."

"You made our search a little bit easier, pretty kitty," the man said with a smile and wink. He leaned in and sniffed her in a deliberate fashion.

At the same time, his mahogany hair drifted over a wide shoulder. She lifted her nose and pulled in the delicious scent of male. Her eyes widened.

It was him!

Her gaze met his knowing one. His fingers brushed her cheek.

"Collin, she's needed inside. We'll talk to her later," the darker-haired male said.

"Don't run from us this time, pretty Luna," the one called Collin said.

Oh, could these truly be the men from her dreams? They were divine specimens. She remembered what he said and shook her head. "No. Not this time. There is no running this time." She licked her lower lip and flicked her gaze between Collin and the darker male. "We?"

"The three of us are we. We dream of you, little one," Collin said.

Melinda gasped at the confirmation of dreams.

"You do as well, it seems. Excellent." Collin grinned at the other male.

"Collin…"

"Right. Sorry. We have a lot to talk about. Luca is right. Now isn't the time because there are lives at severe risk inside. Come, please, Doctor, we're in desperate need for your assistance," Collin said, wrapping an arm around her waist and moving her toward the clinic. "I'm Collin, and this is Luca."

The darker male nodded his head at the introduction.

"Melinda," she said.

"A pleasure to meet you," Luca said in his soft, accented tone. He opened the door for them.

Melinda stopped and stared at the emptiness, the piles of hastily cleaned debris, and shook her head. "Sweet Goddess! You dare to call this a clinic. What kind of a place is this? This is horrendous and inadequate for the size of the clan."

Luca reached out a hand and gave Collin the classic *gimme* sign with his fingers.

"Shit," Collin muttered, yanking five dollars out of his pocket and slapping the bill on Luca's palm.

"What the…" Melinda caught sight of the passage of money between the guardians.

"We had a side bet between us on how fast the person sent would notice the barren nature. I said the moment you entered. He said you would be polite and take a few minutes. I won," Luca said as he pocketed his winnings.

"You placed a bet? On this?"

Luca shrugged. "We're males. We bet on anything."

Collin smacked a hand against Luca's shoulder. "We apologize for our boyish behavior," he said with a growl in Luca's direction, "along with the lack of supplies and quality you'll find within the clinic."

"Why did no one keep up with this?"

"Our last doctor died some years ago, the staff disappeared, and our previous High Alpha didn't give a damn about replacing anything or healthcare. Our new Alpha is doing his best to repair things, but it's taking time. This is one of our first true emergencies where we need a doctor, and one of our females pointed out she isn't giving birth to her cubs without quality care and her crazy mates hovering or passing out," Collin explained.

Melinda's mouth dropped. "Again, what is the reason for the delay in fixing this problem? You knew all of this was inadequate, and no one did anything to fix it? How could this be?"

"Other than the High Alpha, no one qualified is around to make the decision on what to purchase. We have the funds to restock and supply everything, but not the doctor, staff, nor medical knowledge."

"Forget it. We don't have the time to argue the point or me to continue snapping at all of you." She waved an imperious hand in their faces, glanced around the empty space with a nasty growl, and then turned back to them. They both snapped back to attention, and she knew they were checking her out. "Where are the patients?"

"In what we believe are the trauma and surgical suites. Some of the mates brought in laundered sheets, towels, bandages, and other supplies." Collin pointed down the hallway.

"Take me there. Now."

"Yes, ma'am, umm, Doc."

Melinda moved behind them with determined speed and pushed through the swing doors before either one could step ahead. She saw the two large jaguars lying on the gurneys and covered with a white sheet.

"What happened to these cats? Why haven't they shifted back to human form?" She sat her bag down on a counter, pulled off her jacket, and found the stethoscope. She went to the first cat and began a quick, cursory exam. Her nose wrinkled at the smell.

Another powerful male pushed off a wall and stepped toward the gurneys. "Are you the doctor?"

"Yes, my name is Melinda Hurst. I have doctorates in human and veterinarian medicine."

The male ran a worried hand through his hair. "I don't quite know, Doc. I never saw anything like this before with injuries."

"Then I need you to give me the basics of what you know. Where were they found?"

"I don't know the exact placement of their attack. They were out on patrol and ran into a rogue group we've been having issues with on our northern border," the male said and gave her the rundown on what happened.

"Rogues? You have rogues here?" she asked Collin.

"Unfortunately, but yes, there is a splinter group run by, we think, the brother of our former High Alpha. Since the High Alpha's son took over, the rogues have become more active in their attacks and pursuits."

Melinda whipped back the sheet and examined one of the infected wounds. She leaned in and sniffed. She growled at the unpleasant scent. "Some kind of poison is in these wounds. Damn rogues." She lifted her head and stared at the men. "Collin, Luca, I need things from the van," she said and listed the items. "Stat!"

The two men raced off.

"Who are you?" she asked the last male in the room, the one who'd been giving her the explanations.

"Nathan, Doc. I'm a guardian. I sent the others to find these two when they didn't report in on time," Nathan said.

"Good. Fine. You found them, which is the important thing." She moved her stethoscope over one of the cats.

"Can you help them?"

"I think they've been poisoned with something. Right now, they sustained blood loss and are in shock. I'll do everything I can to help them get through this." She went to her bag, pulled out soap and box of blue gloves, and went to the sink. "Do you know anything about medical procedures?"

"I do. I trained as an EMT."

"Good. I need an assistant. Scrub and wash with me and glove up. I don't want either of us to become infected with the poison." She started to scrub her hands with the new bar of soap after getting the water hot and passed it to Nathan, who walked over while rolling his sleeves to his elbows. After she dried off with one towel, she tossed another to Nathan to dry off. She then handed him a pair of gloves to pull on while she slid into her own pair.

"We can't catch diseases."

"We can still be poisoned," she pointed out.

"Which you said is what's infecting their wounds."

"I believe the poison is somehow stopping them from shifting back. Until we cleanse out the wounds and counteract the poison, both men may be stuck in cat form."

"How long could they remain like this before irreversible damage is done?"

"I don't know," she said with a glance at Nathan.

"Zacharias and Grant are two of the best." Nathan moved and stared down at the golden jaguar. "Zach taught Grant and me how to be guardians, along with countless other cats. It's hard to fathom he's the one lying here on the gurney."

"We're back," Collin said as he pushed two rolling tray stands with hooks with one hand. He slung the strap of a large cooler bag over his shoulder and carried another container. Behind him, Luca carried more containers.

"Fantastic. Place a stand by each gurney. Nathan, you can adjust those hooks so they can be pulled out and then raised higher than the tray for the bags," she ordered. She grabbed two other bags from the men and went to another counter. She yanked one bag open and began to pull various contents out, setting them across the counter she cleaned with an alcohol wipe and covered with pads. She turned and held out two razors. "Here, these are electric razors. I believe you all know how to use them. Please remove all the fur on the left arms from the paw to just above the elbow. Collin, Luca, please scrubbed your hands and arms up to the elbows at the sink with the special soap and hot water, use the towels to dry off, and glove up. Then you can use the razors. I need Nathan to help with the rest."

Collin glanced at Luca and back to her. "You want us to help?"

"If we're going to save them, yes, I need all hands on deck with this one. Don't worry. I'll guide you through the simple things while Nathan and I handle the harder routines," she said.

Both men moved to the sink and did as she requested. Once gloved, they each took a razor and went to a different gurney.

"Sorry, Zach man, you're getting a shave," Collin said with a grin. He hit the button and took the razor to the beautifully patterned fur.

"He would be pissed if he woke up with a Mohawk," Nathan said, trying to lighten the tension as he moved to Melinda's side.

"Let's hope he does wake up and gives us some grief," Collin said.

"We'll do our best to make sure it happens," Melinda said and turned to the next set of instruments. She glanced to Nathan. "Do you know the odd thing about shifters versus regular felines is only seen if you know both human and animal biology?" She laid out two IV kits on blue sterile towels.

"Uh-uh. What is it?"

"We don't have to do a central venous line catheter at their neck. We can reach the same veins in their lower arms in either form, so hopefully when they shift, the needles will stay in place."

"Makes life easier."

"It sure does. We don't need to brace their heads and keep their necks stable." She handed him two bags of fluids. "Go and hang these on each stand."

Nathan handled the bags with care and moved.

"Zach is ready for you, Melinda," Collin said as he turned off the razor. He gathered all the fur and tossed it in a waste bin.

"Perfect. We need to get fluids in them as soon as possible." She gathered one kit and brought it over to lay it on the tray. She wrapped the tourniquet high around the upper front leg after she turned it to look at the interior. She tightened the strap, snapped her fingers against the patterned skin, and waited for the veins to appear.

"Have you done this before on a shifter?"

"Hmm, I handled both wolves and cats. I'll need your help on the next few steps, so listen for my instructions," Melinda said as she moved her fingers over the lower limb, searching for the distended subcutaneous veins. When she found them, she kept her finger on them. "Open these packets and hand me one at a time." She pointed out the disinfectant red-and-white packets, which waited with the other instruments.

"I'm here for whatever you need, Doc. Packets, not a problem." Collin ripped open the first packet. He handed her the first alcohol wipe. "It feels strange to do this with gloves. I can't feel anything."

"You get used to it after a while. We can't take a chance with this unknown poison." She used it wipe down the skin over the vein. "Okay. The next one." She tossed the first wipe on the blue towel.

Collin gave her the second, and she repeated the process.

"Good. Open this package," she said and pointed it out. "And hand it to me by the green handle. Do not touch the needle."

With a nod, Collin carefully opened the package and held out the angiocatheter. She took it, pressed the point into the patterned skin until she punctured the vein, and saw the flashback of blood.

"Gotcha. The vein is still strong, which is good. It means his heart is pumping. The poison is slow acting. We have a chance." She blew out an even breath. She advanced the catheter up to the plastic hub and released the tourniquet. She applied gentle pressure to the vein to let it collapse. After she removed and set aside the stylet, she connected the SmartSet tubing, flushing it with a bit of saline to make sure everything worked. Pleased, she taped things in place. She connected the other end of the tube to the bag of fluids and opened the connection. "Okay. There's one. Nathan, bring the other kit over to the tray. Luca, clean the fur from the gurney."

"You got it," Nathan said and carried the IV kit over while Luca removed the fur from Grant's gurney.

Collin moved with Melinda. Since he knew the procedure, he reached for the different packets without her asking for things. She completed the IV in less time than Zach.

"Good work, everyone," she said. "Nathan, clip off the needles and drop them in a Sharps container. You'll find a large container in one of the bags. Again, we need to prevent any kind of contamination due to the unknown poison."

Nathan nodded and went to search for one.

"Is there a rolling stool or something?" she asked.

"Yeah, I think I remember seeing one in another room. Let me go retrieve it for you." Luca moved out of the room.

"Thanks. It's been a long day in the clinic." Melinda moved back to Zach's gurney and studied the view down to his belly and hip, where the deeply infected claw wounds oozed blood and a horrible smell. "Collin, Nathan, what do you smell from these wounds?"

Collin turned to give Melinda a glance and then sniffed deep to take in everything beyond the blood. He pulled his eyebrows together, closed his eyes, and breathed in again. He processed and pulled apart the different layers. "Holy dark moon! What a rancid mixture! It bothers my nose. Aloe. Nightshade. There are a bunch of different lilies, but I can't tell which ones, too many to decipher."

"I'm picking up foxglove, hemlock, and death camas." Nathan shook his head as he blew out a sharp breath through his nose, as if to clear the noxious scents. "It's an odd mix. What the hell did they do?"

"The bastards took everything toxic to cats and mixed it together, but there must be something else in the mixture. There is a base to hold the toxins together and prevent the shift." Melinda went to one of the bags and retrieved a couple of specimen kits. She collected multiple scrapes from each jaguar, labeled everything, and bagged them. She then drew blood into more vials from the catheter for more tests. "I need to run this through the lab. They'll let me know what else is in this stuff." She placed everything in a medical specimen bag. Once she finished, she pulled out things to flush, suture, and dress the wounds. She carried everything over to the tray next to Zach. At the same time, she saw Luca return with the stool.

"Thanks, Luca," she said and had him raise it to the same height as the gurney. She settled with a sigh of relief. "Let's start cleaning these. Nathan, do you want to work on Grant while I take care of Zach? You can follow me. Then I'll close the wounds."

With a nod of assent, Nathan gathered the same supplies and placed them on the other tray. "Lead away."

"First, pick up the squeeze bottle of saline, use your other hand to slightly open the wound, and flush deep with the saline solution. We must remove as much of the infection, blood, and debris as we can. If something is embedded, clean tweezers with alcohol wipes, and use them to pry anything out of the wound. Do this to all of the wounds," she explained. "Luca, could you assist Nathan?"

"Of course, Melinda," Luca said with a nod and moved to help the other guardian.

"Do you think you can create an antidote?" Collin asked.

"I hope I can once I know the mixture of the toxins and the base. Until then, we'll work on flushing this from their systems and see if it helps bring them out," Melinda said.

It took time and careful attention, but Melinda and Nathan cleansed all the wounds of the debris and infection. She put a drain in and sutured them all closed. It took all of them to flip each jaguar before they could repeat the process. In between all of it, they removed and hung new bags of fluids for each cat.

Melinda returned to the bags, took her best guess, and loaded large syringes of high-dosage antibiotics. She pushed both into the catheters for each male.

"I'm not quite sure how to counteract the poison, other than it needs to be flushed out of their system. I'll have to see what the lab results tell me," she said as she pulled off the gloves and tossed them in the medical waste bin. She dropped back on the stool, exhausted from the work.

A soft chuff rumbled from Zacharias, to everyone's surprise, and Melinda moved to stand by his head with the others.

"Hey, big guy, how are you doing?" Collin tugged on the jaguar's uniquely patterned ear in a tender, caring fashion. "You and Grant are back in the valley, safe. You're in the clinic, getting some much needed doctoring and TLC. This is the doc, Melinda Hurst."

Another rumble and chuff came from the big jaguar as his scotch-amber eye found Melinda. His big head wobbled until he could nuzzle his nose against Melinda's hand, and he allowed her to stroke his face and ears.

"Hi, Zacharias, good to have you back with us. You and Grant were poisoned while being clawed. I'm not sure what was in it, but we're working on flushing it out with fluids and antibiotics. Don't try to shift yet, please. Let your wounds heal. Blink if you understand," she said.

The big cat blinked.

"On the off chance, let me ask. Do you feel like you could shift? Blink once for yes and twice for no."

After a few moments, there were two blinks to everyone's disappointment.

"It's okay. We'll figure out why you can't shift. Don't worry about it. Right now, I want you to sleep and heal. I promise I'm not going anywhere until you both are on your paws or feet, whichever comes first," she said and stroked his thick, patterned fur once more.

A heavy purr deep in his throat answered her motion and words. Zacharias closed his eyes and fell back into a healthy sleep.

"Ahh, this is a good sign that he woke. It lets me knows he's fighting and the treatment is working."

"But he can't feel his human side to shift. This is bad, no?" Collin asked.

"It's unusual since our reaction is automatic to return to our human forms when injured or unconscious. This poison is created by another jaguar that is doing something to counteract our base reactions."

"Until we know what they're doing, we're stuck."

"Yes. I'm not well versed in virology, pharmacology, or poisons. If there was someone who knew about this, I would ask them for assistance."

"I'll speak with the Alpha and see if there is someone with the knowledge you seek," Collin said.

"Thank you, Collin. It's a very small field, so the chances are slim." With a sigh, Melinda returned to the stool and sat down hard. "Does either one have a mate? The bond helps with the recovery."

All of the males looked at one another and shook their heads.

"No, both are single," Nathan replied.

"Hmm, it's too bad since the bond magic between partners can be very strong. We'll need to set a schedule of around-the-clock care. Perhaps, Nathan, you could call others and see if anyone else has nursing or EMT training. Maybe they would be willing to pitch in and help out."

"I'll start calling right now. The clan will come together to help our guardians." Nathan moved away to start making some calls on his cell phone then jot notes on a pad he located in a bag with a pen.

"How are they? The truth," Collin asked.

Melinda let out a long breath, slung the stethoscope around her neck, and rubbed the bridge of her nose. "We're not out of the woods until they shift, but I don't want them to with their wounds so aggravated and infected. The shift would help the healing process, but being in the jaguar form accelerates things, too. It's a wait-and-see game now, especially with Grant. We need him to wake and respond to us."

"What about you?"

"As I told Zach, I'm not going anywhere. I need to call the clinic and explain what is happening." Melinda rubbed a hand over the back of her neck. "I wish this place had some damn decent lab equipment so I wouldn't have to return to Paisley."

"I believe I can assist with your request, Doctor," another male called in an authoritative tone.

Melinda turned on the stool and peered between Collin and Luca, who both moved to stand on either side of her in a protective fashion. This move seem a little odd to her, but she enjoyed the feeling. "Hello? How can you do this? This place is a bit of a disaster," she pointed out. "Everything here I brought from the clinic."

"I'm High Alpha Alex Thurston. I believe you would be Doctor Melinda Hurst?" the handsome man said as he moved through the swing doors.

She nodded and rose to her feet. She bowed her head in respect and felt the gentle wave of Alpha power wafting from him. Unlike other Alphas, he didn't try to overpower her, but let the energy wrap around her like a warm embrace. "Greetings of the Goddess, and respect to you, Alpha Thurston."

"Greetings of the Goddess to you, Doctor Hurst. You have my deepest thanks for taking care of my guardians, Doctor. I hope you would consider the honor of joining the Fire Moon Clan as our doctor. I found your application, somewhat belated, among the mess of our files after taking over my father's reign. As you pointed out, we're in desperate need of a doctor and an operational clinic. Perhaps you would consider taking on this challenge for us." Alex waved his hand around the dilapidated mess surrounding them.

"Then there is the other matter Luca and I would like to discuss with you," Collin murmured in her ear.

"The two of you?" she asked, lifting an eyebrow.

He smiled.

"You can talk about personal things later, toms. We require a doctor and working clinic," Alex said with a shake of his head.

"What? Didn't do nothing," Collin said, a look of innocence on his face.

Luca whapped Collin on the back of his head.

"Thank you, Luca," Alex said.

"Welcome, Alpha," Luca replied.

Collin rubbed his head.

Melinda snickered along with Nathan, who chuckled while he moved to change the IV fluid bags.

"What do you say? We can move you into one of the houses. There is a place near the clinic or on the outskirts, whichever you would prefer. I would bypass the temporary status and proclaim you an honorary member because of our desperation," Alex said.

"Not to mention it would get Hillary off your ass," Collin said.

Again, Luca whacked the back of Collin's head.

"Ow!" Collin rubbed his head again. "Knock it off."

"Then shut off the smartass remarks," Luca said.

"Are they always like this?" Melinda asked, pointing at the duo.

"They can be worse," Alex said, "but they're harmless." He looked at the guardians and then back to her. "No matter what their behavior, I can't deny they're two of my best guardians. Collin is actually the leader of them, and Luca is his number two."

Melinda turned the stool and stared at Collin. "You're in charge?"

"Yup. Imagine my surprise when it happened," Collin said as he rocked on his heels.

"Well, shit." She glanced at the Alpha and back to Collin and Luca. "They both know what happened."

"Yup."

"What about my coloring?"

Collin shrugged again. "Yup."

"Shit…" Melinda looked to the ceiling and blew out a long breath.

"I apologize, Melinda, but I can't hold secrets from my Alpha and partner," Collin said. "Nor did I know anything else about you at the time. I wanted to find out who you were."

"It's all right, you didn't know my concerns," she said.

Alex held up his hands to try to calm her. "You have nothing to fear from me or anyone else, Melinda. I know of the rumors and the myths concerning a Luna. No one will ever force you to serve in such a horrible way against your will."

"It's why I left my home clan. Please don't call them for a reference. I don't want them alerted to my location," she pleaded.

"Did someone there try to force you?" Alex moved to crouch in front of her.

Melinda felt a warm palm press against her back and glanced over to see Collin had stepped closer to offer quiet strength and comfort. She leaned against his side and felt his fingers move down her spine in a gentle caress.

"Melinda?" Alex asked.

"The High Alpha…" She swallowed hard at the memory. "He believed the myths. He wanted me for himself and a circle of his guardians as a sex slave to empower them."

Luca growled in a fierce undertone. His hands clenched into fists.

Melinda noticed how his knuckles turned white from the power of his strength. She reached out and placed a hand on his forearm. She saw his gorgeous green gaze drop to meet hers at the light touch.

Luca dropped with ease to one knee next to her. One hand unclenched, and his fingers brushed against her cheek. "Did they touch you?"

"No. A guardian friend alerted me and helped me pack what I could in my SUV. I escaped in the dead of the night without telling anyone, not even my parents. I tossed my phone and headed here after making a false trail to a different clan," she said.

"Very brave of you to make such a difficult decision and change in your life," Alex said. "Things wouldn't have been much better if my father was still in charge, though. Good thing he didn't see your application or notice your arrival in Paisley."

She gave him a wan smile.

"Damn the dark moon, Alpha. This is one of the reasons we need an overseeing council beyond local ones to remove those Alphas in control." Luca growled.

Alex nodded. "An Alpha Conclave is formed, but not known, Luca. They work in secret, behind the scenes. I learned about them when they called me shortly after I took office."

"What?" Luca and Collin asked at the same time.

Melinda's eyes widened.

Alex lifted a hand. "I can't say more, other than I will pass a message to them about your former Alpha, Melinda."

She nodded.

"Could you return to my request about becoming our doctor? Again, I offer a clan, a home, and full honorary membership," Alex said, holding his hand out for a shake.

Melinda put her hand in his larger one. "I accept. I want full control over the clinic."

"Welcome to the clan, Doctor Hurst. This place is yours to do with as you desire. I believe Collin or Luca have a full-access credit card to purchase supplies and whatever else you need to get the lab equipment. Feel free to create a rush order and have it delivered overnight to the valley."

Alex rose to his feet.

"Would they do it?"

"I believe with the amount of money we'll drop, they will. If not, pass them along to me, and I'll give them a talking to. You'll get what you need within the next two days, if not by the morning."

Melinda's mouth dropped as he walked away. She looked at the guardians. "He really means it?"

"Oh hell yes," Collin said. "When he says something, he will finish the job."

"Anyone have a laptop?" Melinda asked with a chuckle.

Chapter 5

It took a few hours, but Melinda ordered everything she could possibly need to reequip and stock the clinic either on the laptop or by telephone. To her surprise, everything would be delivered within two days as Alex promised, three at the latest, since some equipment was large and a little cumbersome to bring into the valley. She requested a sanitizing crew to come in and give the entire clinic, from the top floor down to the main, a full ceiling-to-floor deep cleaning and sanitizing before the supplies and equipment arrived. The patients would be covered and moved as needed. At Collin's urging, she also ordered computers and a telephone system. She sighed and looked around, imagining what it would appear in a few days with everything she ordered in place.

Collin watched her walk away but let her move without his shadow. She knew she wasn't leaving.

"Should we bring her to the house for our talk or move to another place in here?" Luca asked as he stepped next to Collin.

"She wouldn't want to leave her patients unattended, but we'll make the offer."

"She's beautiful," Luca said while his fingers trailed over Collin's hip.

"Yeah, she'll be a powerful, stubborn mate. One we'll need to take tender care of so she doesn't overwhelm herself." Collin looked to Luca. "We'll offer her courtship, like Raphael and Sebastian. Though, we may add in the sexual relationship, unlike them, if she desires. Unlike Hillary, I feel more passion riding in Melinda. No matter what we may request, the answer would be in her hands. She is the one in control, not us."

Luca nodded in agreement. They turned when they saw Melinda walking back toward them.

"Okay, everything is ordered. I called my old boss and let Jim know I took on a new job. I mentioned when he hired me, I was waiting for a call from the clan. He knows about our kind since jaguars are seen," Melinda said as she pocketed the phone. "He was upset, but he understood my choice. He requested I cover the morning shift to give him time to bring someone in, and I said I would as long as the patients here were being watched. I figured it's the least I can do for him on such short notice. I mentioned he would be compensated for the supplies I took for the case."

"Not a problem at all," Collin said. "We'll let Alex know, and he'll have his admin team cut a check to Jim."

Melinda rubbed a hand over the back of her neck. "I take it now could be the time for our talk."

"Unless you're too tired, and if you don't mind, there is much we wish to discuss with you," Collin said with a sheepish grin.

"No, I'm good for a little longer. I know we need to talk."

"We can talk here, find the office or somewhere to sit, or we could drive to my place. I can offer a warm meal, coffee or tea, a shower if you wish, and a warm bed."

"Let me check in with Nathan and the cats. I think we should talk in private at your place. Not to mention, I could use a good meal and shower. I've been at the clinic since dawn."

"You had a long day and can use a little TLC. I believe we can provide you with some simple pleasures," Collin said with a glance to Luca.

"Sounds like a plan to me," Luca agreed.

Melinda returned to the surgical suite with Collin and Luca following. They were all surprised to find four females and two males standing and talking with Nathan.

"Ahh, there she is. Doctor Melinda Hurst, these are the first of our volunteers," Nathan said and introduced the other jaguars. "They all had either nursing or EMT training. We moved the rest of the necessary supplies from the van inside and began to do a little organization around here. We'll also work on the cleaning issue."

"Excellent. I called in a specialist crew to give everything a good sanitizing to medical standards before all the equipment arrives. I welcome you to the clinic and thank you for your assistance in this crisis. If none of you have jobs, perhaps you would consider working with me at the clinic," Melinda said as she nodded and picked up the stethoscope. She moved to the two sleeping jaguars and gave them another check.

"I filled them in on the situation and potential issue with the poison. We'll make sure everyone knows to wash and glove before touching anyone. They know how to change bandages, check for infection, and replace the IVs as needed," Nathan said when she finished.

"Good. Nathan, I'll leave you in charge and please create a rotation for the watch. I don't want them left alone. See what you can do about bringing in some cots and blankets, along with food and coffee."

Nathan nodded.

"I need to leave for a bit and speak with Collin and Luca. Collin, can Nathan call your phone if anything changes? I need to return to the clinic for a morning round and bring back the van. I'll have to pack up my personal things at some point." Melinda glanced back at Collin.

"Of course. Nathan knows the number," Collin said.

"Don't worry, Doc." Nathan waved toward the guys. "I'll keep an eye on them. Get some rest. You did one helluva job."

"Not finished yet, Nathan. We need to figure out what's in the poison mixture and how to counteract the effect. Keep an eye for the crew and get them to work as soon as possible. Have someone watch their work so nothing is missed. Then there will be multiple deliveries of supplies and equipment. Find a couple of large rooms, have everything placed there, and create an inventory list as you receive them."

"Not a problem. I can do all that. I'll look up some forms to create everything we need and print them out. We'll be fine, Doc."

"I know how to handle inventory and forms, Nathan," one of the females said. "I can assist with that part."

"Wonderful. I want to thank you all again for coming to help." With her instructions finished, Melinda removed the stethoscope and handed it off to Nathan. She picked up the white coat and a smaller bag.

Collin moved his arm around her shoulders and left the room with Luca. He helped Melinda enter the passenger side of the Paisley clinic's van. "I'll drive this one back to the cabin. You can rest."

"Oh, sounds good." She pulled out the keys and handed them to him. Collin closed the door, walked around front, and slid behind the wheel.

"I'll see you both at the cabin," Luca said through the open door before he closed it for Collin. He tapped a hand against the window, walked off to his truck, and then got behind the wheel.

"Here we go," Collin said when Luca pulled out and drove away from the clinic. He backed out the van and followed him down the street.

The ride to Collin's home was silent. No one wanted to be the first one to speak.

Luca parked in front of Collin's home, which was turning into his home as well, and they all got out. Collin parked the van next to the truck and turned off the engine. He got out, moved around to the passenger side, and helped Melinda down. He took her hand in his and led her to the door and inside.

"Talk first or food?" Collin took her coat and bag. He tossed her keys in the dish on a small entry table by the door where Luca also placed his keys.

A long yawn escaped Melinda while she looked around and then found her way to the living room. She curled up at the end of the sofa and stared at them.

Luca glanced at Collin as he closed the door and followed her. He settled on one of the armchairs while Collin sat on the other end of the sofa. "I say a warm shower and food for the doc. You did mention this was a long day for you," Luca said.

Hiding another yawn behind her hand, Melinda nodded. "Sorry. The adrenaline is disappearing."

"Then we'll give you some TLC first. Come with me, Doc. Luca, do you wanna scrounge up some dinner for all of us?" Collin said as he rose to his feet and took Melinda's hand to help her stand.

"One yummy dinner, check," Luca said, pressed a kiss to Melinda's cheek, and headed to the kitchen.

Melinda touched her cheek as she watched him leave and lifted her gaze to Collin. "And us?"

"I'm taking you upstairs to the master bathroom. Do you have other clothes?" Collin led her through the house.

"No, I didn't bring another set of scrubs."

"I'll pull out some sweats for you, then. I think I have a pair with the drawstring attached."

"Considering our differences in height, yes, a drawstring would be handy," she said with a soft chuckle.

"Here's the master bedroom," Collin said, opening the door at the end of the hall to reveal the rich wood furniture and simple earth tones for decoration.

"Simple, but comfortable," she said as she trailed a hand over the forest-green quilt.

"Creature comforts," Collin said with a chuckle as he pointed the way to the bathroom. "I don't have girly scents for shampoo and body stuff."

"I don't mind. I'm so used to antiseptic smells, I will take anything else." She stepped inside the large bathroom, staring at the double vanity done in rich granite, the hidden toilet, a sunken garden tub with Jacuzzi nozzles, and the extra-large walk-in shower. She moved to the shower and stared at the multiple showerheads and the control panel on the outside. "You have a programmable shower?"

"Yeah. It's the best investment I ever purchased. There are six heads, which can move all over, with varying pressures and temperatures," Collin said as he hit the panel.

"Ohhh. I may not get out of this shower until I'm a prune," Melinda said with a laugh. "I want it almost hot, and strong pulses like a massage."

"Take whatever time you desire. I had a larger heater installed."

"If we didn't have to talk, I would sink into the tub for an endless bath."

"Next time you can indulge," Collin said and programmed her shower. "Okay. Hit start when you're ready." He pulled a pair of towels out of a closet and hung them over some bars. "These are warmers."

"No way…"

Collin grinned at her simple pleasure and couldn't wait to give her more. She was right, though, they needed to talk before she left for the animal clinic. "I'll let you get to it then. Enjoy."

"I will," she said and turned to him. "Thank you, Collin."

"No need to thank me," he said and kissed her cheek. "I'll leave some clothes on the bed. Then we'll see you downstairs for dinner and our talk."

"Okay."

With another glance at her, Collin forced himself to leave her alone in the bathroom. He gathered some clothes he hoped would fit her and left them as promised. Then he put his feet ahead of one another to move downstairs.

* * * *

A little over an hour later, swamped in the overlarge sweats, her hair fluffy from a quick blow-dry, and a delicious dinner in her belly, Melinda tucked her feet underneath her as she curled against the corner of the sofa. She held a warm cup of chamomile tea in her hands. "Okay. No more avoiding what we're all here for and time for the talk. What do you want to tell me? Other than our day in the forest, this remains a little embarrassing to me."

"All of the sudden, I have no idea what to say to you," Collin said as he settled on one end of the sofa, a mug of coffee in his hands. "Any way I think about what to say…The situation would sound crazy as hell to you."

"Crazy…" Melinda chuffed as she blew against the steam and took a sip of tea. As she moved, the locks of hair fell past her shoulders, tumbling unhindered. "Guardians, I know all about crazy situations. I happen to be one of them in flesh. I'm a damn rare Luna female who some believe is a myth and Goddess-blessed. I escaped from my previous clan. I kept my cat a secret from my parents and others as long as I could. Somehow, the High Alpha found out about me."

"So you left your home clan," Collin said.

"After my friend explained what he heard, there wasn't much choice about staying. There was a plan to capture me after one of my runs and transformations while I was still vulnerable, and of course I would be outnumbered. While on the run, my guardian friend and I made it appear that I took off in one direction for them to follow. Instead, I headed across the country to here. Things didn't go according to plan when I ran into a dead end of sorts since I heard nothing about my application." She lowered her gaze to the cup of tea before taking another sip.

"A good thing you didn't hear back from our previous High Alpha. Knowing the bastard, he would try for the same damn thing. It's what Alex was trying to tell you earlier."

"I heard him, but didn't believe…" Melinda moved and lifted her gaze to stare at him with wide eyes.

"Don't worry, please, and you'll have no trouble from him. Alex would never let anything or anyone harm you, nor would we," Luca said.

Coughing on his coffee when Luca nudged him mid-sip, Collin cleared his throat. "Yes, yes, sorry. What a stupid thing for me to say. I didn't mean to worry you," he reassured her. He set the mug down and placed a hand on her knee. "You have nothing to be concerned about with the clan under Alex's rule. His father was sent to another council or even this Conclave as a prisoner. He did a lot of damage to our clan and some members, and his son is making sure he pays for it with his life after a trial."

"And his son?"

"Alex. You met him."

"He seems like an honorable sort of a jaguar."

"He is and more. He's rebuilding our clan and wants to provide the members what they need to thrive and create more opportunities. A lot is on his shoulders, but we're trying. A lot of the infrastructure under his father was never created or continued."

Setting her cup down, Melinda dragged a hand over the back of her neck and through her hair. "What is happening between us? I mean…" She swallowed, glanced at the cushion, and rolled a lock of hair around a finger. "I know what happened in the forest…It was a heat thing, right? Both of us were aroused by the chase, nothing more."

"Yeah, umm…Perhaps a little more than a heat," Collin said with a glance to Luca. "Luca and I are…Crap, how do I put this?"

"He's trying to tell you we're mates pulled together by scent," Luca said, not sugarcoating it.

"The two of you," she said and pointed a finger between them.

"Yes, but our mating isn't the two of us. Something special in our clan is happening, a blessing by the Goddess."

Silent, Melinda waited and listened.

Luca glanced to Collin, who nodded and let him continued. "We're the male members of a potential blessed triad mating."

"Triad?"

Luca nodded.

"With me?"

This time both males nodded.

Melinda opened her mouth, lost her words, closed her mouth, and sat dumbfounded.

"Did we lose you?" Luca asked.

"Umm. Not lost, but a little shocked. This isn't something a girl would get asked every day."

"Yes, we're kinda figuring out how to do this."

"I can see."

"We would never ask you to leap straight into an unknown mating, let alone a triad mating. The males of our first triad recovered an ancient law of courtship from the library and reenacted it to court their lady," Collin said.

"Courtship?" Melinda said, reduced to single-word questions from the shock.

"It allows us to focus on a stronger connection between souls and hearts before the physical one."

"Physical one?"

"Sex. He means sex," Luca said.

Melinda shifted her gaze between them. "What about sex?"

"Umm. Well…The ancient law mentions once a claim is put in writing, proclaimed to other members of the clan, and certified to the High Alpha or elders, sexual activity up to intercourse is allowed.

Only intercourse or penetration isn't allowed. Depending on the members who sign up for courtship, some have decided to rework the ancient law concerning sexual intercourse. They always take in the preference of the female within the mating. No one will take advantage of her."

She pushed another hand through her hair, stuck a finger between her plush lips, and nibbled on the nail. The males were silent as they watched her actions with care. "This is a very interesting law. What else did they do?"

Collin patted Luca's knee and leaned toward Melinda. "It's an interesting story about Sebastian and Raphael. They were in a monogamous relationship for years and neither one participated in the seasonal dances, which ended up becoming forced sexual pairings. Most fought against the dance and pairing while others took advantage." Collin glanced to Luca, who nodded. "Then they saw their chosen, Hillary, and how she was being treated, and found a way to change everything."

Luca continued the story. "Since then, Sebastian created a registrar office for potential couples and triads to announce their courtship to the clan, which is the first step. The office also provides support and advice for them, as well as overseeing all to make sure everyone honors the laws."

"Are things still in the beginning stages?" Melinda asked.

"Yes, the entire clan is figuring out the courtship, the laws, and how to announce things. Everyone is on a learning curve. The seasonal dances are completely gone. Alex forbade them as soon as he took office. No one can be forced into a pairing."

Melinda leaned back, nibbling on her finger once more.

"All we're asking for is a chance, Melinda. Collin recognized your scent as his potential mate. This is why you were drawn to mate, even in shifted form. When he returned home, I almost ripped into him when I smelled you. Not only were you his plausible mate, but mine, too. Both of our cats rose, possessive as hell, but we realized we were another triad," Luca said, his hand gripping Collin's knee. "Neither one of us could believe it when it happened."

"If the scent turns out to be wrong and things go bad between us…" she ventured.

"We'll remove the claim and step back from you. You'll never have to worry about us forcing ourselves upon you."

"I…" She licked her lips. "I need time."

The males glanced at each other and then back at her.

"Understandable. We probably threw you for a loop with all of this information," Collin said.

"Yes, I need to figure out… Beyond what my cat desires, I need to think about the rest of me."

"Of course. We understand."

"No, you don't. For so long, I needed to hide the truth of who I am from everyone. I'm a Luna. The name is surrounded in mystery and myths, all of which impacted my life. Now I sit here with you two, one of you has seen my cat, the other hasn't, but both of you accept and know about her, my biggest secret."

"What do you mean?"

She nibbled on her finger once more and shook her head. "I have no clue. I'm never in this position."

"Then we shouldn't add pressure and should give you the time you request to consider the offer," Collin said.

"You would do this?"

"Of course. Females are in charge and have all of the power within the courtship ritual," Collin said and rose to his feet. He held his hand to help her stand. "Though, we do ask one simple request of you."

"Which is?" she asked while standing, her hand still captured in his.

"We wish to do an exchange of scents between the three of us. A true exchange."

"Not the simple brush we did earlier at the clinic," Luca added.

"Oh, well, okay. I guess I could allow both of you to keep my scent. I don't see the harm of this, especially with the threat of rogues," Melinda said.

Collin stepped closer and released her hand, only to take hold of both her shoulders. He brushed his cheek against hers, felt her satiny, smooth skin warm against his bristled skin, and knew he left his mark on her face, until his nose bumped to her ear. He held the position, shifting a little to give Luca room.

Luca stepped in against Collin's side and wrapped his arm around Melinda's waist. He slid his cheek against Melinda's other side, marking her with his bristle, until his nose met her ear, too.

Trapped between them, Melinda pressed a hand against each powerful chest. She pulled in a shaky breath as their mixed scents surrounded her. Desire swamped her body while arousal flooded her panties with moisture.

With slow, deliberate attention to exquisite, sensual detail, each male breathed in her special unique scent, which bloomed behind her ears. The burst of nerves and glands helped to bring the essence forward.

As their warm breath wafted against the supersensitive spots, Melinda shuddered with pleasure and arousal. A soft moan lifted from her lips. She turned to sniff behind the ear of one male and then the other. Her inner feline growled, yowled, and paced faster inside her as she recognized each one as her potential mate. Her cat stretched and pawed in her mind, wanting to claim these men. Now she could always find them among the entire clan by scent alone, even in shifted form.

Luca drew his fingers down her arm, coved in Collin's sweats, but she felt every trace of his touch. He nuzzled her again, softer, in a fashion to let her know they felt her arousal and need. He let a chuff escape.

"Oh, sweet Goddess, I...I can't..." She shook her head, feeling her confidence shattering since she was so unsure of herself in these unknown situations. "I'm so sorry. I must go." She pushed and wiggled out of their arms and raced to the door.

"Wait, Melinda, please…" Collin said as he turned and held out a hand.

Luca turned and pleaded with dark eyes.

"I can't. Call if anything changes with them. I'll return later. Sweet Goddess, forgive me. I'm sorry," she said, snatching her bag, pile of scrubs, and keys from the dish, and she shoved her feet in her shoes.

"Melinda…"

* * * *

They couldn't do anything more than watch as she fumbled her way out of the door, pale hair streaming behind her as she climbed into the van. Both of them reacted in time to rush out the door, out into the cool night. Standing on the porch, they could only watch as the van drove away.

"Crap," Collin muttered.

"Yup," Luca said.

"Did we screw up?"

"I don't know."

"Now what are we going to do?"

"I have no idea. Our lives and our hearts are all in her hands."

Collin leaned against Luca and let out a grumbled sigh.

Chapter 6

Trembling by the time she pulled the van next to the clinic, Melinda dropped her head on the steering wheel. "Stupid, stupid, stupid." She banged her forehead against the wheel with every repeat. Two gorgeous toms wanted her forever, and she ran away like a chicken, afraid they would be like all the other men who coveted her supposed powers. She yanked the keys out, climbed down, and dragged herself into the clinic. She stepped into the small office, closed the door, and sat. With a few deep breaths and some simple meditation, she tried to clear the lust and exhaustion from her mind and body for a few more hours. Her cat yowled, demanding to return to their potential mates, but she closed her down.

"No, I can't let nature overrule me, not now and not at this point in my life."

Her cat snarled, but Melinda ignored her inner feline.

"I can do this. Take one step at a time, Melinda. Do your job," she ordered herself.

Rising from her chair, she stripped off the overlarge sweat suit, which had Collin's scent in the fuzzy, warm fabric. She laid them over the bed, intending to wear them later, and tossed her bundled bloody scrubs in the laundry bin. From a drawer, she yanked on a fresh pair. She shoved her feet in a different pair of socks and shoes, pulled her hair back in a high ponytail, grabbed a stethoscope from her desk, and went out to the clinic. Though she didn't tell anyone she was returning tonight, she decided she needed the energy and endless, simple love of the smaller animals to ground her after Collin and Luca.

When she finished the night appointments and checked on the overnight patients, Melinda noticed it only took two hours. Mumbling about how slow time moved, Melinda tossed the last clipboard on the desk. Since there was nothing else to occupy her night, Melinda locked the clinic, set the alarm, and trudged up the outer stairs. She pulled Collin's sweats back on, wanting to keep the scent around her as she slept. She dropped forward on the unmade bed, kicked a sheet over herself, and drifted into a restless sleep.

It wasn't the damn alarm clock that woke her mere hours later, but the screaming alarms of the clinic and the dogs barking in their cages. She heard the yowls and cries of a vicious cat fight scrambling outside.

Melinda raced to the door. She yanked the door open, stood on the small landing, and stared down in fear at the fight. Three large toms cornered a golden jaguar against the clinic's back wall. The golden cat continued to snarl against his attackers in spite of his injuries and the odds against him.

"Come…Come…Enough of this fighting, Luca. You can't win," a man said as he appeared out of the forest. His voice was silky smooth, but dark and full of evil.

Melinda crouched to blend into the shadows. She pressed a hand to her mouth. *Luca! No…*

"I know the Luna is near the valley. My toms caught her scent while she hunted last moon. Give her to me, and perhaps I'll give my nephew the antidote. I believe this is a fair trade, one little female for two lives," the man said.

Luca snarled in reply.

"Fine. We'll find her on our own. She can't hide forever, not with a rich scent surrounding her subtle power I can taste in the air. I'll have her by the next moon, but you'll never know. You'll be joining your friends." The man raised a silver tube and blew.

Luca yowled when a feathered dart hit between his belly and hip before he could move. He dropped to the ground.

"Return to the forest. Leave him to the humans. The poison will kill him, like the others," the man said to other cats. Within moments, they slipped into the forest and disappeared.

When Melinda couldn't hear them, she raced to Luca's side. "Luca…Luca…Sweet Goddess, no, not you." She found where the dart entered him, but noticed how it went straight through a fold of skin. The point didn't enter his muscles and empty its poisonous contents into his bloodstream. Unlike the others, she hoped he would have a better chance at recovery. She was careful when she yanked out the dart.

With a yowl, Luca managed to shift back to human, but she could see how it hurt him from the way he cringed and his body rippled and contorted. He wheezed for breath when he finished. "Inside. Get me inside."

"It went through a fold of skin. I don't think you got a full dose."

"Still on their claws. I feel some of the stuff coursing through me. Inside…Safety. Must get inside. Please, beloved."

"Sweet dark moon, I don't want to watch you fall into their clutches. Not when we barely got a chance to learn about each other."

"Inside. Must get inside," Luca insisted.

"All right. Stubborn fool."

"Protective stubborn fool. Now…Inside."

With a sigh, knowing he wouldn't stop insisting until they moved to the safety of the clinic, Melinda pressed the code to turn off the screaming alarms. She saw the broken glass panel on the door.

"Sorry… I had to alert you…only way I knew to set off…alarm," Luca said between breaths as he rolled to his hands and knees.

"Don't worry. It's happened before. Kids have thrown rocks. Don't. Let me help you." Melinda rushed back, wrapped an arm around him, and supported his heavy weight with her strength. "On three…" She grabbed the dart and then counted and helped him on his feet. Together, they stumbled through the door and inside the separated room. She got him to lean back on the treatment table.

"You need to close…door… Hit both the deadbolt and lock… Alarm. Don't forget…to turn alarm…back on. May come back if hear sudden stop… Get suspicious and check…"

"Okay. I will."

"No." Luca shook his head. "Now…I'm too damn weak to fight them off…not until we flush this crap from my system, if we can. It may be too late. I'll end up like the others."

Melinda went back to the door, threw the deadbolt and locks, and reset the code. For good measure, she found a block of wood they used before and tucked it against the smashed glass. "Good?" She returned to his side, gathered supplies, and opened packaged gauze, pressing some to a vicious wound. "Luca… What happened?"

"Don't have much longer…Feel poison…Bastards dipped their claws before they attacked…I watched them." Luca licked his lips.

"I'll heal you."

"I know." Luca lifted his bloodied fingers to her sleep tousled hair. "My mate."

She nuzzled her cheek against his fingers, not caring about the blood. She captured Luca's lips in a soft kiss, her tongue hesitant as she found the seam. She licked against his full lips, felt the heat of a fever, and pulled back. "Tell me what happened."

"How I wish I had more time to kiss you," Luca whispered and groaned. "On patrol. Splinter group followed me. They wanted you and smelled you on me."

"I heard them. Why me?"

"Don't know. Luna. Something about Luna." He pressed a hand to his temple. "Dizzy. Fight started back on trail…Collin…No…" His gaze became worried.

"What? What about Collin?"

"He'll see blood and worry. I know him. He'll want to track me down, but could run into them. Call him."

"I will after I take care of you."

"No, must call him and tell him to return. He can't go after them."

"I will call. Let me take care of you."

"Sorry I brought them here… Clinic was closest during attack… Got befuddled with poison…lost my way."

"I'm okay and they didn't see me. I'm glad you found me. I can start the treatment right away before it settles much deeper inside you."

"Collin…Call…Splinter group…Robert Thurston…" he whispered and dropped to one knee. "We know he led, but the bastard is active in poison creation. Somehow…can't figure out everything. Damn. Sweet moon…I feel so weak."

"I will, Luca, I promise." Melinda caught him under one arm and hoisted him upright once more. "I need you to get on this table. Come on, one more push." She helped him leverage his weight and then stretched him out. "Good. Let me go calm the other animals and get some supplies. I'll be right back."

"You need to call Collin."

"I will. Hush. Rest."

"Poison…It calls to my cat…" Luca shook his head.

"Luca, don't leave me. You need to stay with me." She leaned over the table, smoothing her fingers through his hair.

"Can't fight any longer, my sweet. I'm sorry. It's too strong." He lifted his heavy eyelids and stared at her. "So beautiful. My mate. Wish I could know you better."

"You will. This isn't the end for us."

"I'll be like others. Gone and trapped inside my cat with no way back."

"No, I'll figure out the damn antidote myself. I'll heal you." Leaning down, she brushed her lips against his mouth and found his lips dry and chapped. So different from their first kiss, he didn't respond to her. "Luca…Stay with me."

"Wanted to taste you one time, like Collin…When you were in the forest…How I want to make love to you, show you the other side of mating. How we could spend hours, Collin and I, teaching you all about our love."

"You will. We'll have our chance to make love." She touched his cheek. "Would sex give you energy to fight the poison?" She moved her fingers down his chest and belly, avoiding the horrible clawed wounds. Her fingers wrapped around his semi-flaccid cock.

His eyes closed at her touch. "Melinda. Too late…My cat comes…" He pushed her hand in time before his body contorted in agony with the sudden shift. All the loose bandages fell away from the wounds as they reopened with the shift.

Surprised at the unexpected shift, cursing under her breath, Melinda slammed her palm down on the table. She ignored the sting in her palm, but welcomed it as the pain brought her back to herself.

Panting with exertion, Luca opened one bright-green eye before he closed it and slid into an exhausted sleep.

"Rest, darling. Let me take care of you," Melinda said, stroking the soft ear. She opened the door into the back treatment area for large animals, separated from the smaller pets. First, she moved to the in-house patients, soothing the barking dogs and the meowing cats. Then she retrieved various treatment items and returned to Luca.

She gathered all the used gauze and tossed it away. She found the dart on the floor where she dropped it after helping him inside. After she picked it up, she studied and sniffed the tip. She caught the same scents that were found in the wounds on the other jaguars.

"Oh, Luca…Please, I hope you didn't get the full dose."

Knowing what was needed, she gloved her hands and moved into automatic action to give him a large IV to begin flushing out the poison. Then she cleansed and sutured the multiple wounds. Once Luca was comfortable and treated, she yanked off her T-shirt and changed in clean scrubs, socks, and a pair of Crocs. Dressed, she rushed upstairs to the apartment to find her cell phone. While she raced back downstairs, she dialed the number Collin gave her.

"Hello, Thompson here."

"Collin, it's Melinda," she said as she entered the room where Luca slept.

"Melinda, hi. I'm sorry, but things are a little crazy. Can I call you later?" Collin said.

"Wait, don't hang up. I know…It's about Luca."

"Luca? What do you know about Luca?"

"He got trapped by a rogue group between the valley and the clinic. Three cats cornered him alone in a fight, ripped him pretty good, and chased him to backdoor of the clinic."

"Oh, holy dark moon! We only found parts of the bloody trail, but it got scrubbed. Where is he now? Is he…"

"There's more. A man appeared and ordered Luca to turn me over to him in exchange for the antidote. Luca refused. He shot him not with a gun, but a dart. Collin, the dart is filled with the same poison. It managed to go through a fold of skin and not in his muscle. I don't know how much he received, but he saw one of the cats dip claws in poison before they sliced into him. He's fighting some of the poison."

"A man spoke with Luca? Did you see this man? How did Luca tell you this in his feline form?"

"Yes, I saw the man who led the attackers and taunted Luca. I have Luca here in a back treatment room. He managed to shift to human form and talk to me before his cat took over. He said the man is called Robert Thurston, and he's been in charge all along. The man knows I'm a Luna. I heard him say it."

"Holy dark moon! May the Goddess forgive me, but fucking hell!" Collin cursed. "I knew something was wrong. I could feel it inside me."

"I started the treatment same as the others, but until I figure out what the poison is and the antidote—"

"There is a chance he'll be like the others."

"Yes, it depends on how much he received. I'm hoping it isn't as much, but with his reaction there is no telling. You need to speak with the Alpha and warn everyone. No one can go out alone. Especially the children and not even the guardians are safe against this."

"I will speak with Alex, I promise. I'm sure he is going to suggest the same when he listens to all the details. We'll set patrols closer to town to make sure no one else gets harmed."

"Good, I will feel much better."

"You said Thurston wanted you in exchange for the antidote. He knew you are a Luna? How?"

"He said they caught my scent when I hunted last moon. I know I have a unique scent and traits, but I thought the smell of an entire clan would cover me since I tracked behind some of your known trails."

"Why would he want you specifically? How did he learn you were in town other than your shift?"

"I don't know."

"Did you recognize him?"

"No, but he may have heard of my existence from my previous High Alpha."

"You need to return to the valley."

"I will after today's appointments."

"No…Now."

"I can't. Please, Collin, I keep my promises and commitments. At sundown, come in Luca's truck with another guardian or several, so you can lift Luca and the medical equipment to the back. Then I'll need someone to drive my SUV and things after you or with another guardian for safekeeping while I stay with Luca during the ride."

"You can't stay at the clinic alone. I'll send a guardian now. He'll come by cat, but stay as human. He's a black jaguar with blue eyes and his name is River. After the Alpha heard about the situation, he requested I pull River into things and help you. He knows his way around a lab as well as a guardian. Don't open the door until he knocks in this pattern," Collin said and sounded out the knocks.

"The Alpha chose him for lab skills? I don't understand…never mind. I'll ask him when he gets here." Melinda didn't understand, but went along with what Collin said. "Okay. I'll look out for him. Keep everyone safe over there."

"We will, and the same goes to you and Luca. Keep him alive, please."

"I will, I promise." She closed the phone.

When she moved back to Luca's side, the great cat opened his eyes, licked her fingers, and chuffed.

"Yes, I called Collin. He's worried, but staying put. He's sending a cat named River to keep an eye on us," she told him.

Luca nuzzled her fingers again and fell back to sleep.

"Okay. Guess we can trust him." She caressed his ear once more, sat in a chair, and fell asleep next to the golden jaguar.

The repeated, oddly patterned knocking pulled her out of a restful sleep. She snuffled, rubbed her face against her arm, and opened her eyes to find tawny fur covered with black rosettes. Melinda blinked and pulled her head back to get a better view.

"Oh, shit, Luca. Forgot what happened…" She rested her hand on his chest, felt his heartbeat and breathing, and let out an even sigh of relief.

The knocking at the back door pulled her attention from Luca. She remembered the call to Collin and how he told her about a cat coming to guard them. This was River's knock.

"River, sweet Goddess, I'm forgetting everything now." She pressed the alarm code and released the deadbolt. She cracked it open to see a tall, ebony-haired, deep-blue-eyed man dressed in rumpled khaki pants and T-shirt standing outside. "Who are you?"

"River, ma'am. Are you Doc Melinda? Are you taking care of Luca?" the slender jaguar said. "Collin sent me. I've been knocking his pattern for about ten minutes now."

"Yes. Yes, I'm so sorry. I fell asleep. Come in, please." She backed away and opened the door further to let River inside. "You didn't see any other jaguars out there, did you?"

"No. Other than the two jaguars that came with me from the clan and raced back to the valley. They didn't know I would be standing out here. Collin doesn't want anyone to travel alone." River stepped inside and watched her reset all the security measures. He saw Luca stretched out on the examination table. "Sweet mother moon." He moved to his fellow guardian and studied him. "I didn't know they were this bad off. Never saw anything like this in my lifetime."

"I doubt any one of us ever seen such treachery. He's stable. I'm using the IVs to flush his system, like the others at the valley clinic. I'm using the machines here to begin preliminary testing on samples I gathered. I hope to get some idea of what we're dealing with concerning this damn stuff," she said to reassure him.

"I guess that's why Collin sent me with the Alpha's regards."

"Why do you say this? Collin said the same, but I couldn't figure out the cryptic message."

"I think you asked for someone with my expertise to help out with this situation to Collin, who spoke with the Alpha, who hunted me down in my lab. I'm Doctor River Essex of virology and pharmacology," River said.

"You're a doctor?"

"Not a medical doctor, so I could never treat any patients. I run a small laboratory in the valley. I don't get sent on guardian errands, but Collin and High Alpha Alex were insistent I come here."

"Oh, thank the moon." Melinda jumped and wrapped her arms around his neck to embrace him.

River chuckled and hugged her back.

A low snarl broke them apart.

Melinda turned her head and saw Luca open his eyes to see them embrace. "Oh, shush. River can save your butt, silly feline. Back to sleep."

"Your mate?" River asked.

"Possible. Along with Collin," she said.

"Triad?"

"Possible."

"Impressive," River said.

She managed to unearth an extra pair of flip-flops for River to wear from a stockpile of useless stuff in a storage closet. "Never know what you can find in this closet. Use these for now. Let me get the tests results."

"Thanks," he said as he stuck his feet in the thongs. "Odd shoes. Prefer loafers in my lab. For the duration of the day, all things considered, I believe it'll be best for me to stay back here."

"Considering most are humans out there, I think it would be best. I'm going to make sure they don't enter this area." She nuzzled Luca's face, brushed a hand over her hair to reassemble her human-front at the door, and left the room. She noticed techs were starting the morning rounds and procedures.

"Morning, Doc. Heard this is your last day," the senior tech, George, said as he checked on a beagle.

"It is, George, and I'll be leaving to head my own clinic."

"Congratulations, but I'm sorry you're going. I know everyone will miss you."

"I will miss you and everyone else. It's been a pleasure to work here."

"Shall we get going? There are some potential ICU cases in the overnight area to be checked. I made a note of which ones we need to attend first," George said as he lifted the daily sheet on his clipboard.

"In another minute, I need to do one more thing. Let me pick up some test results and bring them to the back room where I have a private large animal case I don't want disturbed, and I'll be back in for morning rounds. I don't want anyone to enter the room and get accidentally bitten or clawed. I'll handle the case myself," she said.

"Ahh, good idea to use that room since you can keep the case isolated. While you get the results, I'll put a note on the door."

"Thank you." She moved on to find her papers and lab work. Moments later, she handed them off to River, explained how to change the various bags on the IV, petted Luca, and grabbed her coat and stethoscope to leave for her last day.

With George at her side, they performed a check on the overnight patients in both cat and dog sections and the large animal area. She made her notation on their charts after checking their vitals, injuries or illness noted, and their current well-being after the night. She flagged those who were ready to go home and others ready for the next step in their care. Of course, as George noted on his clipboard, there were others not doing as well. Once she agreed with the notes, she motioned for George to call other technicians to move them to the ICU area, where they began extra treatments to give those beloved pets more care while she went to call their respective owners about what they wished to do about continuing treatment.

The roughest part was speaking with a heartbroken owner who wanted to do everything humanely possible to save their pet, but sometimes finances, the animal's overall quality of life, or time wasn't an option. Other times it wasn't in the best option for their pet.

Melinda took the time needed to speak with each owner about their furry beloved and their best options, noting the answers on the charts before she went back to the ICU. Two were made comfortable until their owners could come in for final good-byes. The other three were going to try to be saved with further measures and she gloved up to do her job.

In between appointments throughout the day, she stepped into the room with Luca and River. She checked his bandages and overall well-being. She spoke with River about the test results and, at his request, sent another sample of Luca's blood through the machines for a different test along with what was left in the dart.

During another break, she sent George to the store for the largest chunk of meat available and two extra-long stacked deli sandwiches for herself and River. When he returned, she went back to the room and tried to feed the meat to a sleepy Luca, who wasn't appreciative of the prepared meat.

"I know, picky cat, but it's all we have. You need to keep up your strength. Try to eat something," she said, holding her palm flat with the chunk of beef next to his muzzle.

"Isn't the IV giving him nourishment?" River asked around his sandwich.

"Yes, but we're cats. I want to give him more than liquids if he takes it. It's the same with the others."

Luca sniffed and lapped it from her palm before giving it a chomp and swallow.

"There's my guy. Here's another." She placed another chunk on her hand.

He repeated the lapping procedure.

"Good kitty," she teased and praised.

He chuffed at the nickname and licked her palm, his tongue rough against her sensitive skin.

She giggled at the feeling and helped him finish before she enjoyed her sandwich. She caressed his head while she discussed the poison, possible antidotes, and treatments with River.

"I'm leaning toward a heavy-metal poisoning base. Since we're talking about us, I'm going to venture a guess that the combination is liquid mercury and silver. This will be the base," River said as he held out the recent report.

"Shit. Either one is nasty, but together, they're lethal if they enter the bloodstream."

"Yes, which means they want the dart system. It would apply the poison directly into the bloodstream faster than the claw method. I believe in the earlier attacks, the claws were dipped in the mixture, but during the fight, some of the mixture was removed before it could be delivered. Though the dart is deadlier, they would need human hands and mouth or a gun."

"They need to test the methods."

"Yes. They have the poison, but not the delivery system. A point in our favor, but not the best."

"It could allow us a little time to figure out something to counteract the attacks."

"For how long," River said.

"True."

"You're right about the plants. All are toxic to felines, and the combination is lethal. Whoever concocted this is…"

"Is plain evil, with a madman in charge." She shook her head as her gaze went down the list. "Do you have any ideas of possible antidotes?"

"We'll start with what you're doing and flush the bloodstream. We'll follow with a chemical balance, something with a charcoal base to counteract the metals. I'm leaning toward a chelation therapy, but I need to figure out which chelators and amounts will work. When we return to the valley, I'll take blood samples, go to my lab, and begin to work on the treatment."

"I heard about this treatment. They use it for acute heavy-metal poisoning."

"This is basically what we can treat, so attack it first. If the therapy pulls out plant toxins, then we're on the right track."

"Good plan, River."

"This is what I'm good at, since I'm not much of a fighter," River said with a lopsided grin.

"Once the morning is done, we're out of here. I'll need to throw a few of my things in suitcases and boxes upstairs and carry them to my SUV, too, before we all leave. I don't have many belongings."

"We'll deal with it when Collin arrives."

Melinda nodded, kissed Luca's forehead, and returned for her next round of appointments.

Chapter 7

After signing off the last of her paperwork and her exit papers, Melinda shook hands with Jim and left the office. She shook hands with some of the other techs and even accepted a few hugs from some who were teary-eyed. With a long breath, she stepped into the back room and found not only Luca and River, but Collin and another, even taller male with shaggy brown hair falling over his eyes.

"Collin what is all…" She moved a hand around the filled room.

"Melinda, there you are. Ah, hello, darling," Collin answered with a sheepish look. He moved to take her in his embrace. "I'm sorry. I couldn't stay away any longer. I needed to rush over here and make sure both of you were safe."

"How did you get inside?" Melinda snuggled close as her arms looped around him

"Sorry, I believe that part would be my fault. I memorized the code when you let me in and I have a tendency to remember signals," River said, waving a hand.

"Ahh, it isn't a big deal. Jim will change it as a security precaution once I leave." She nuzzled her face against Collin's neck for his warmth. She lifted on her toes and initiated a soft, simple kiss between them. She touched fingers to his cheek as she met his gaze. "I'm happy you're here."

Collin kissed the tip of her nose. "I wanted to come earlier. How are you holding together?"

"A little tired, but under the circumstances, not too bad," she said. "Thanks for sending River. He unlocked a lot of the mysteries. We think we can counteract most of the lethal portions until he can figure out the antidote."

"Can you do this?" Collin asked River.

"Yes and I need to take some samples of everything, get to my lab, and begin some tests. We have some ideas that should work, though there is something called a chelation therapy that will clear the heavy metals, but I need to figure all the numbers and factors. There are steps to help slow down and prevent the dangerous aspects. Melinda began the most important part by flushing with the IV fluids and the wounds," River said.

"Good. This is good. Whatever you both can do, you have the Alpha's full assistance and approval. Though, I know when possible, Alex will want to you to keep him updated about your progress on everything," Collin said.

They nodded.

"How is our guy?" Collin stepped to Luca and caressed the soft ear. He leaned over and pressed a kiss above Luca's closed eye, rubbing his finger along the length of Luca's snout. "Luca, hey there, love, I'm here."

Luca's eyes opened, and the pupils contracted until the green irises focused on Collin. He chuffed and moved to nuzzle Collin's hand.

"Hey there, love. Decided to take on a trio of nasties all by yourself, huh, big guy?"

Luca grumbled and nosed Collin's hand. His tail flicked low.

As discussed earlier, Melinda found a bag of a liquid charcoal mixture. She mixed it with her hands, hung it from the IV pole, and connected it. "Okay, Luca, this stuff might make you feel queasy. This is liquid charcoal and will combine with the silver and mercury. I'm hoping it will help neutralize to pass without damaging your liver and kidneys." She moved an empty bucket to the table. "River, in case he needs to hurl."

"Why me?" River asked.

"I need to pack. I want Collin to come with me for security since I don't know the big guy over there," she said, pointing a thumb to the jaguar by the door.

"Gideon, Doc. I'm called Gideon Ashbury," the male said in a deep, burly voice.

"Gideon, hello. I'm sorry, but I would prefer one of my two mates," she said.

"I would prefer it as well, since we're territorial around our mates," Gideon said with a smile under his shaggy hair.

Collin snarled at the taller jaguar.

"As you see, I like keeping my paws attached," Gideon said with a deep chuckle.

Melinda smacked Collin in his stomach. "We'll be down in a little bit. Keep an eye on Luca. If he becomes fidgety, pale in the gums, or anything unusual, get me."

"Understand, Doc," Gideon said as he opened the door for them.

Collin took the lead, used her key to open the door, and checked out the apartment before he let her go inside. "What if the charcoal mixture doesn't work?" he asked while he followed her through the open floor plan. Near the bedroom area, he pulled down the suitcases when she pointed them out in the closet and then built the boxes she tossed him.

Melinda placed the suitcases on the bed and began to fold and place her clothes inside in a haphazard fashion. "As River said, this is a temporary measure until he figures out the chelation therapy. Until then, we need this mixture to neutralize the metals. Since they're in a liquid form, we can't pull them out like we could if they were bullets or arrows. They need to be encapsulated or dissolved in another mixture that is nontoxic and can be removed. In regular dogs and cats, we use charcoal to force them to throw up or gather the poison."

He sat on the edge of the bed.

"Collin?"

"I...Sweet moon, I never found myself so scared as this morning when I heard about the blood and Luca missing, and I heard your voice. Your wonderful voice telling me Luca was with you. Only he wasn't." He lifted his gaze to reveal ocean-blue irises filled with fear and worry. "Can we lose him? I can't, Melinda. He's a part of my soul, my heart, like you are. This is tearing me apart."

"Oh, Collin," she said, moving to him and settling on his lap. She wrapped her arms around his shaking shoulders as she held onto him. She felt his arms go around her, hanging on to her like she was the safe port in the swirling storm of his mind. "We're not going to lose him or any of them. I swear to you, Collin. On my life, we're not losing them."

Collin let out a shuddering breath, almost a cry, as he dropped his head against the crook between her neck and shoulder.

"He's strong. So strong and has mates. We'll feed him energy."

"Mates?" Collin whispered.

She placed her hand on his cheek. "The full moon rises in two nights. Together, we can bring him through the ceremony before the Goddess and become mates."

"You said..."

She stopped him by placing her fingers on his lips. "I was an idiot for leaving the both of you. I'm saying yes."

"Don't do this to save his life."

"I'm doing this to save my life."

At her words, he leaned in and captured her lips in a heated kiss.

"Finish packing. We need to get out of here and get you and Luca home," he growled against her lips.

"Agreed. I need you to get to work on the living room."

"Living room?"

"Yes, darling," she said, using her hand on his cheek to turn his head. "I need to put all the books in the boxes. Then I need you to use the stack of newspaper on the coffee table to wrap the knickknacks and place them in another box. Can you do all this for me?"

"Yeah, sure. What about you?"

"I'll take care of my clothes and bathroom stuff."

"Furniture?"

"The furniture stays here. Also, could you pack the laptop and peripherals in another box?"

"Good. Nice list. Keep me busy, occupied, and my mind off Luca's condition. Can't worry about losing Luca," he grumbled as he lifted her off his lap, stood, adjusted his thick bulge, and walked away.

"We're not going to lose Luca." She went back to work on her clothes. Part of her prayed the idea of them becoming full mates in the eyes of the Goddess would work at least for Luca's sake. She didn't know about the other cats lying in the clinic.

Within a couple of hours, they were on the move back to the valley. Melinda was surprised to find two more jaguars standing outside the back door, one next to her SUV and another next to Luca's truck. Both nodded.

"Earlier on the phone, you mentioned how you would like to ride in the back of the truck with Luca and me. I would have River drive your car with one of them as guard, and Gideon will drive the truck with another as guard," Collin said.

"It was a suggestion. You don't mind if I stay out in the open and not tucked inside?" she said.

"Against my better wishes, I figured you would prefer to be with your patient, and I'm staying back there with you."

"You would be right. Everything is tied down for the journey so nothing is jostled," she said as she hopped in the back.

"Yes. We set you up with a cushion and tie-down as well," Collin said as he followed her up and helped her secure herself.

"There's been no vomiting. Seems he's taking the treatment well," River said as he closed the back.

"Wonderful," she said as she checked the half bag, which was on a lowered pole. She petted the soft fur. "I hope the trip doesn't bother him." She unlatched a set of keys and tossed them to River. "Leave these inside on the table for Jim. He'll know what to do with them."

"Will do, Doc. Car keys?"

She tossed him the key fob.

"Thanks." He caught it out of the air. "I'll take care of your baby."

"Please do. She's been through a lot."

River jogged back to the clinic to do as she asked. He got into the driver's seat and started the engine to signal to Gideon that he was good to follow.

Collin banged on the window to indicate that they were secured. Gideon drove away. Collin reached out over Luca to take Melinda's hand in his as they left. "Sorry we're leaving your old place like this."

"It's okay. I knew I would leave one way or another, so I didn't turn it into my home. It wasn't permanent," she said. "Being in a good clan with a mate is permanent, a dream."

"Now you get to live your dream."

"Hmm. I never thought I could, but you and Luca came along and are helping me realize it, but you and Luca came along and are helping me to realize it. Not only that, but now I have my own clinic to help heal others."

"Though this isn't how you would want to start healing, with a rogue group setting out to poison us." Colin dropped his hand to touch Luca.

"No, never in my dreams would I think someone would be vicious enough to turn on another in such a cruel fashion."

A jostle caused Luca to snuffle and open his eyes. He yawned and licked his lips.

"Hey there, love. We're on our way back to the valley. Hang in there a little longer, and we'll get you into the clinic with the others. Nathan is setting up another comfy bed for you near Zach and Grant," Collin said as he moved his hand through the thick fur.

Luca let out a soft noise and nosed Collin's arm.

"You're going to be okay. We promise," Collin said.

"In two days, the full moon rises, Luca. Collin and I will help you dance before the Goddess and pledge our mating," Melinda said.

Luca moved his gaze to her.

"I'm saying yes, Luca. I'll mate you and Collin before the Goddess. I'm hoping that our love and energy, along with the Goddess, will help heal you."

Luca closed his eyes and rested his head on Collin's lap.

"I don't know if he approves," Collin said.

"Why not?" Melinda said.

"To change your mind to save him. He wouldn't want to put you in that position," he said.

"I'm..."

Collin shook his head as Luca chuffed.

Melinda fell silent.

Chapter 8

Once Luca was settled on another gurney, all IVs situated and secured, Melinda hooked new charcoal solution bags to the others after River took his samples.

"I promise to return as soon as I get the results and order what we need. We'll need to keep them under careful watch throughout the therapy since it is dangerous," River said as he placed the samples in a small container.

"Hurry, please," she said.

"I'll give you a ride to the lab, Doc," Gideon offered. "My truck is outside."

"Thanks, Gideon. I appreciate it." River followed the bigger man from the treatment room.

"Hey, Doc, how are you doing?" Nathan stepped into the room to assist Melinda. "What do we have going on here?"

"Hi, Nathan. I'm tired and worried about Luca and the others, but hopeful we're on the right path and with what River is figuring out," she said and explained to Nathan about the charcoal treatment and possible symptoms for each jaguar so he could add it to their files. "Any change in the others?"

"Grant woke yesterday, early in the morning, and was able to react to questions, like how Zach did. They've been coming around off and on since then. We gave them hand-fed chunks of fresh meat. Neither appreciated the offerings, but they ate," Nathan said.

"Yeah, Luca was the same," she said with a chuckle.

"We're hunters. We don't always like raw meat dropped on a plate. It's not part of our internal nature as felines."

"Or males," she teased. She moved to examine the other males, gave each a light caress when they responded, checked their wounds, and noticed the fresh bandages and flushed drains. "How are the drains working? What have you been finding?"

"Last night they were filled with the same infection, blood, and pus. Their bodies were trying to push everything foreign out of their bloodstream and heal. The wounds continue to bleed."

"It's normal for us to bleed until they heal and fresh blood means we're sending new platelets and cells to the diseased flesh. Make sure the bandage changes remain constant. I sutured the wounds in a light fashion to make sure they didn't bleed out."

"Would we need to remove the sutures later?"

"Once the wounds begin to close, we'll pull the drains and clip the sutures. I hope we'll see their natural healing aspects take over."

"Gotcha."

"How were the drains this morning?"

"The amount of pus was lower, the smell of infection less, but noticeable."

"So the therapy is working, but we haven't cleansed them. Between the charcoal and chelation therapies, we should remove the heavy-metal poisoning."

"Heavy metal?"

"Silver and mercury."

"Shit, they were the base?"

She nodded.

"Also deadly to jaguars and we should have realized they would use such metals."

"Don't blame yourself for this. We're not to blame. The rogues are." She placed a hand on his shoulder and waved one of the females over. "I'm sorry, what is your name again?"

"It's all right, Doctor. The meeting was brief and late. I'm Laura Haywood. Sebastian's one of my cousins," the young brunette with a warm cocoa-brown gaze said.

"Laura, hello and thank you for being here," Melinda said to the gentle female. She paused and lifted an eyebrow. "Sebastian... Isn't he one of the first triad?"

"Yes, that's him. He's been over the sweet moon since he and Raphael found Hillary, and now they're expected cubs. He's practically dancing everywhere. With a beloved cousin as a guardian, I wouldn't be anywhere else when one of our protectors is in trouble."

"Cubs? Their mate is expecting cubs?"

"Yes, Hillary is pregnant with triplets. They've been overprotective, and I think she's about ready to deck them. I can't blame her." Laura giggled at the thought.

"How much longer does she have to go in her pregnancy?"

"I believe she has another two and a half months left."

"With our shorter gestation time, she could be due in another two to three months. We're between five and six months instead of the normal human nine-month span. I need to see her," Melinda said as she made some rapid calculations in her head. "Are there other pregnant females?"

"Yes, I know of several others, along with some who gave birth. We have a pair of midwives, but they're elder females who witnessed many births."

"I need to create an OB-GYN and pediatrics wing within a rapid time frame," Melinda said.

"We'll pull in whatever resources you need. The crew was here earlier and sanitized everything. All the debris is gone. Most of your equipment and supplies are here," Nathan said. "We'll need to find Annabelle, who kept a detailed inventory and offered to become your administrator."

"Annabelle? Perfect, we need to find her." Melinda stretched her neck from side to side as she went through a mental list. "Okay. Laura, could you keep an eye on them? I need to see the changes with Nathan and find Annabelle. Did you listen about the possible symptoms to the treatment?"

"It would be my honor to stay. Yes, I overhead the conversation."

"Good and any changes, please call for us."

Laura nodded and settled in for the long vigil.

"We'll start the tour this way." Nathan opened one of the doors after Melinda caressed Luca before they left the room.

"Who is Annabelle?"

"She's a half-blood of a guardian and his human mate, one of the rare cubs who couldn't shift upon reaching adolescence."

"I know about half-bloods, something about a faulty gene. There're more females than males."

"It's something else I believe River is studying. A way to help half-bloods regain their jaguars, if they desire."

"Is she trustworthy?"

"Oh, yes, I've known her since we were cubs. Our fathers are good friends and guardians. She's mated to another guardian, Miles, who adores her."

"Good to know and thank you. I'm sorry for the questions, but we'll be dealing with the clan's personal information. Everyone will be questioned and scrutinized."

"Understandable. I can ask the Alpha for a suggestion about any background checks you require."

"They would be helpful to have, though I don't want to put more work on his desk."

"He mentioned any help you need, he would put through first. He's anxious to get the clinic running as soon as possible."

"I don't blame him. Even though we rarely fall ill, our cubs are as vulnerable as humans until they reach adolescence and their first shift. Even our elderly can become susceptible if they're not careful."

"We've lost a few elders since the clinic closed. It's been hard," Nathan admitted.

Melinda growled under her breath at the unacceptable loss of life.

Nathan touched her arm for a moment, redirected her through the altered clinic, and showed off all the changes that happened since she left the previous night. They went to the front waiting room. Melinda stared at the pale-blue painted walls, several paintings, and then the low-backed wraparound sectional sofas that sat around the perimeter. In the center, several chairs were placed back-to-back in a couple of rows, tables between the sofas and chairs, and coordinated lamps.

"I didn't… I forgot about this… How?" She moved to the sofa, touching the soft leather fabric to reassure herself this was real.

"One of our guardians noticed all the deliveries, and his wife dragged him inside. She demanded to know what was happening, so I explained like a good tom," Nathan said with a grin.

Melinda sat on the sofa.

"The lady looked around at the front room and how it remained empty, and she asked about what your plans are. I mentioned you didn't order anything, concerned first with the equipment and supplies. She set this big shoulder bag down, pulled out a pad, pen, and measuring tape and went to work. As she worked, her husband wandered over to me, closed my jaw, and mentioned his wife was an interior decorator and they'll be handling the front waiting room as a gift."

"They did all this in a morning and afternoon?"

"A lot of hands went into the project. I believe Juliet is returning with a bucket of donated toys for a cubs' area in the corner, some magazine holders and stuff, and other items. I think. She wanted to talk to you about helping you change the upper floors and the rest of this one. Basically, she wants to help transform the entire clinic with your permission."

"Oh my sweet Goddess," Melinda said, tears tracking down her cheeks as she looked around.

"Doc?" Nathan asked. "Uh-oh…" He looked around, helpless when it came to female tears. "Umm. Collin! Collin!"

"What? What," Collin called back as he jogged from a side room where he had disappeared to talk to other guardians.

Nathan waved his hands toward Melinda.

Collin spun to see what distressed the youngster and chuckled. "If you can't handle a female in tears, cub, don't look for a mate."

Nathan growled.

Collin went to Melinda's side, sat on the new couch, and gathered her in his arms. "Hey there, ssh, beautiful lady, what are all the tears for? Nice digs you got here."

More waterworks burst forward at Collin's words.

Collin tucked her head under his chin and rocked her with care and tenderness. "Mel, sweet Mel, what... What did I say?"

"They don't even know...me...and look. Look what she did." Melinda waved a limp hand around.

"Who doesn't know you? Who did what, sweetheart?"

Melinda cried harder against Collin's chest.

"Nathan, explain," Collin said.

"I told her about Dawson and Juliet's visit. Juliet recreated the waiting room and wants to do the rest of the clinic," Nathan said as he wrung his hands together.

"Then what happened?"

Nathan waved his hand toward Melinda. "Waterworks."

Melinda sniffled a teary chuckle. "Overwhelmed by such generosity by strangers," she said. "I never got such a reaction from my old clan. Juliet doesn't know me."

"You're a doctor who is rebuilding a clinic and coming to our aid. It's all she needs to know about you, darling. She knows you have a wonderful heart," Collin said.

"Until they see..."

"No, don't think such a thing. You don't know how anyone will react until the moon," Collin said. "We'll deal with it at the time."

"I can't mislead them."

"We're biding our time to get through a crisis."

Melinda nodded against Collin's chest. She brushed the tears away and pulled back.

"Okay now?"

"Yeah, I'm sorry for the breakdown."

"Let's see…In the past two, almost three days, you were yanked from your regular veterinary job to assist two jaguars knocked out by an unknown poison, had two more jaguars announce their intentions—I'm sure you had a little sleep—were wrenched out of sleep by alarms and a catfight to find another wounded jaguar, treated him along with numerous other patients at your old clinic, and were dragged back to the valley for more drama," Collin listed. "I think you're due for a little crash of nerves or minor breakdown."

"Considering how you put the last few hours, yeah, I'm overdue."

"I'll make sure to schedule some sleep for you tonight. Your SUV will be at my place along with you, in a separate bedroom if you desire. Anything you need from your car?" Collin winced and rubbed his neck. "Ugh, that sounded like an order, not an offer of help or support."

"No, it shows you care for me." She shook her head and smiled. "I don't mind the order to stay with you. I don't want to sleep alone in an empty place, unless I would crash here to keep watch. I would like the suitcases and bathroom items along with my laptop."

Collin smoothed a hand over her hair, noticing she had tugged it into a braid at some time during the day. "I'll make sure they're waiting for you in the guest room."

"I'll take the guest room for now. Is there any news from River?"

"No, I asked Gideon to remain with him for both security and communication, since River can get lost in his work. Gideon will contact me when River finds something."

"Okay. I need to finish this tour with Nathan."

"Want me to go with you?"

"No. I'm better now. This is a strong, generous clan," she said.

"We're stronger under Alex. He's making us better every day he's in charge." Collin kissed her gently, thorough in his attention. He left her breathless and flushed by the time he rose and left her alone with Nathan.

"He…Oooh…" She growled at his retreating back.

"Going to get him back later?" Nathan asked.

"Sweet Goddess, yes." She banged a fist on the soft cushion.

"Good for you."

Smoothing a hand over her tumbled locks and feeling that some had escaped the braid from Collin's fingers, Melinda rose, took another look at the gift, and gestured for Nathan to finish the tour. Part of the tour was finding and speaking with Annabelle, who was thrilled to speak with Melinda about everything that had arrived in the clinic.

Hours later, the three of them leaned over a table in another room, old blueprints spread out, layouts of all the floors, and lists of which areas were needed. They needed to accomplish a lot to get this clinic functioning.

The door burst open, and Laura stood there breathless.

"Laura, relax and breathe. Tell me what happened," Melinda said.

"Two more…Guardians brought in…" Laura swallowed hard as she caught her breath. "Two more attack victims."

"Oh no, not more guardians." Melinda and the others raced back to the treatment area.

"Not guardians." Laura grabbed at Melinda's shirt. "Not guardians."

Melinda stared at the female. "Then who? Only guardians should be out during this crisis. Everyone else is ordered to stay inside."

"A pair of adolescent cats. Teenagers. They snuck out."

Melinda paled and slammed a hand against the nearest wall to brace herself.

"Who are the teens?" Nathan asked.

"Dawson and Juliet's daughter and her boyfriend," Laura said, tears in her eyes. "My cousin said they announced their courtship under the new law this past weekend."

"Juliet…The one who decorated the front room," Melinda said as she picked up her pace.

"Yes," Laura said as she and Nathan followed.

"How was the poison administered?"

"Dart. The guardians brought in the darts," Laura said.

"They have a better chance. The darts seem to administer a slower dosage than claws." Melinda pushed through the doors and saw two more beds filled.

The teenagers were in human form, breathing heavy, and writhing with some pain. The young female's long brown hair fell almost to the ground in a braid tangled with leaves and grass. She put up some kind of struggle, along with her boyfriend. Melinda lifted the sheet covering the young male and found a few light scratches, but nothing deep or infected.

"What were they doing outside the town's limits?" Melinda demanded. "Didn't the Alpha put out the word to everyone?"

"Yes, Doctor, but…They're teenagers, reckless and foolish," one of the guardians said. "We found them by an abandoned cabin, a place where the youngsters go when they want to hide their doings from adults. We patrol it to keep an eye on them."

"We found them lying a few feet from a blanket and picnic. Both had the darts in their hips and backs. Two each," the other guardian said.

"Damn." Melinda cursed and stared at the young female. "Foolish kids…"

The girl moaned and lifted her eyelids with obvious effort. "Mama…"

Melinda looked to the others for the answer.

"We notified Dawson, and they're on their way," the guardian said. "The boy doesn't have family. Dawson and Juliet took him in when they noticed their daughter's attention and intention to court. He's a good kid, Doc."

"They're idiots for not listening to orders."

"Mama…" the girl moaned again. "Hurts…"

"Get two IV setups, Nathan. We need to flush their systems," Melinda ordered.

"What about the charcoal solutions?" Nathan rushed around, pushing the guardians to a different wall and out of the way.

"It isn't working. Not making a damn bit of difference. Our only hope is the chelation therapy. Anyone hear from River?"

No one answered Melinda, who cursed low again.

"Bree! Bree, baby," someone shouted in a fearful tone.

"Mama…" the girl whispered.

Melinda looked as a dark-haired female raced into the treatment area with a powerful male behind her. They rushed to the two gurneys, stared down at the patients.

"Bree Anne, baby, what did you do? You knew not to leave the house," Juliet scolded her daughter as she gathered the girl in her arms.

"Mama…So sorry. Thought cabin safe…Parker tried to protect…" Bree said, crying against her mother's shoulder.

Melinda moved to the young man, who was unresponsive to the point where Melinda became worried. She took the IV kit and set up next to him.

"Any response from him?" a gruff voice asked next to her shoulder.

Melinda noticed it was the man, Dawson, who stared down at the patient. "No, he hasn't wakened like your daughter. I think he received a larger dosage."

As they spoke, Parker writhed, opened his voice in a silent scream, and shifted to his golden jaguar form, smaller than the other male cats in the room. He breathed heavily after the shift.

"Parker! Parker! No!" Bree cried out, reached a hand toward her boyfriend.

"Damn. That was fast. I think they changed something," Melinda said to Nathan, as they moved to prepare one of the paws for the IV unit.

"How could he change and not her?"

"I don't know." Melinda's movements were smooth and efficient, and soon Parker was connected to fluids.

"Mama…" Bree called out, and it ended in a screech as she writhed and shifted to her small jaguar form.

"Bree, baby…" Juliet called back, petting her daughter's furry face.

"It's part of the poison. It forces them into jaguar forms. We're not sure why," Melinda said. "Please, I need to shave her arm and place an IV port. We need to start the flushing."

Juliet moved to the head of the bed, not taking her hands from her daughter as she watched Melinda shave the fur then slide the needle in place and hook the bag of fluids to the pole.

"I know it's the wrong time to speak to you. I wanted to thank you for what you did in the front waiting room. It's beautiful," Melinda said in a small comforting tone.

"I'll help you do the rest. I'm not leaving the clinic until Bree does," Juliet said.

"Juliet, what about our other cubs? We need you at home," Dawson said, placing a hand on his mate's shoulder.

"Bree needs me with her," Juliet said.

"During the day you can visit, I promise," Melinda said. "Right now, return home with your mate, comfort your other cubs, and stay safe. There is plenty of support here, and they need their sleep. The moon is almost full and will begin to affect everyone."

"How can we shift with the rogues out there? No one will be safe," Juliet said.

"I don't know. I'm sure the Alpha is trying to figure out a solution. Know I'm caring for your daughter and Parker, and we're working toward a permanent antidote. River is working on the samples in his lab."

"River Essex?" Dawson asked.

Melinda nodded.

"Good. He'll help figure things out. He's smart. Damn smart."

"Sounds like you know him," Melinda said.

"My triplet brother," Dawson said. He held his hand out to Melinda. "Dawson Essex. I'm a guardian, and this is my wife, Juliet. Thank you for coming to our clan."

"Doctor Melinda Hurst, and you're more than welcome," Melinda said and shook hands with the guardian.

"Dawson, Juliet, I heard from my guardians. I'm so sorry they escaped through the security line," Collin said as he rushed into the treatment area. He placed a warm hand on Dawson's arm and glanced at the newest patients.

"As am I to hear about Luca. I would never expect anyone to take him down," Dawson said as he glanced at the other jaguar.

"He was outnumbered and cornered," Melinda said.

"Why is this bastard doing this to our clan?" Juliet demanded.

"Why does Robert Thurston do anything? Power. Greed." Collin shrugged and placed his fingers against Melinda's back when he lied about the reason.

"I want this bastard under my claws," Juliet said. Her hands clenched in tight fists.

"We all want the same," Collin promised.

"Until then, we keep supporting our patients and searching for a cure," Melinda said.

Chapter 9

The almost-full moon hung heavy in the sky as Melinda crawled between the soft sheets. Instead of staying in a guest room, she was in the main bedroom with Collin. She wanted to feel Collin's strong arms around her. She didn't get away from the clinic since three more guardians, scratched, wounded, and shot with darts, were carried into the treatment center. They placed patients in two rooms, nurses kept vigil throughout the rest of the evening, and guardians stood around the perimeter.

Melinda murmured as she fell into a hard, deep sleep of exhaustion.

River couldn't get the chelation therapy to work on jaguar blood and poisoning. He said it worked with normal human blood, but after adding the jaguar genes, something didn't work. He wasn't giving up, but it would take longer than he thought.

Melinda wasn't sure how much longer the jaguar patients had, and she worried. Grant and Zach's stats were beginning to lower, and she knew one or both would soon fail. It was a matter of time before any lingering poison would overwhelm their systems.

She didn't want to return to Collin's home and sleep, but Collin, Nathan, and the others all insisted. They needed her in top form, and it required a solid bit of sleep and food, and Collin provided both when they entered his home. Until the clinic was finished, it was hard to get everything or everyone comfortable except the patients.

Wrapping her arms around a pillow, Melinda murmured and drifted away into dreams. She found herself standing in an open field, dressed in a flowing, almost-sheer white gown, barefoot, her hair loose about her back. In the center was a fire pit and bowers of trees, and it appeared to be the center of a clan's moon gathering place. She stepped through the cool grass and looked around.

"Hello?" she called out, hoping Collin or Luca would appear. She needed them.

The full moon sent down a single column of pure light in the center of the fire pit at her voice. From the light, a figure emerged, dressed in a billowy silver robes with a midnight column dress underneath. Her hair, as pale as Melinda's and covered in sparkles, tumbled around slender shoulders then down her back. The female smiled as she moved on silent bare feet.

"Greetings of the moon, my daughter," the female said as she stopped. "You grew up gorgeous, as I knew you would."

"Greetings of the moon, Mother Goddess of the Moon," Melinda said and sank into a low curtsy to the Goddess of all jaguars.

"Rise, my special daughter." The Goddess touched her on the shoulder.

Melinda rose as bidden.

"You are the daughter of my body, my flesh, Melinda. A true daughter of the moon. A Luna jaguar with many special gifts," the Goddess said, curling her hands around Melinda's face.

"Daughter…Your daughter? But…how?"

"Every three generations, I choose a clan to gift and strengthen. First I give birth to a white jaguar and give her to a prominent family to raise and nurture her as their child until she is grown. When she can change form and is fully accepted by her clan, I can appear to them."

"But the Vernal…"

"Yes, my daughter, I chose poorly and I apologize. They turned away from me under the deceit and rule of their High Alpha. As did the Fire clan under their previous Alpha, but I saw the potential for change in the Fire, and I didn't see it in Vernal. I managed to reach a guardian to assist you."

"Is he all right? Is he safe?"

"Yes, my daughter, Phillip is safe. I have future plans for him."

Melinda relaxed, her concern for her friend soothed. "Oh, I was worried for him. Worried what the others would do when they realized how he helped me flee."

"His path was altered the moment he listened to his dreams."

"But, Mother…" Melinda smiled, as the name now meant so much more to her. "The Fire…I'm not accepted and they haven't seen my other form."

"They will on the full moon."

"The moon…Oh sweet moon, we can't shift and hunt! The rogues, the poison…It'll be devastation upon everyone," Melinda said, her hand moving to press her fingers on the Goddess's forearm, finding it silky and warm under her touch.

"I will protect my Fire Moon Clan from the dangers."

"I can't cure them. The therapy doesn't work for us. I don't know what to do, and I'll lose Luca…I know he is my mate, one piece of my heart. His loss will destroy Collin and me. We must take him through the dance and your fire."

"No. He cannot step foot in the fire. None of them can touch my fire," the Goddess warned. "They are weak, and my fire will take them to eternal rest. They will not pass through my fire."

Melinda's knees wobbled at the Goddess's words. "The dance… Collin and I are…Oh sweet Goddess…We could have killed him?"

"It is why I am here tonight. No dance except for you. You will step forward and shift as I appear to the Fire clan."

"Shift to my white jaguar in front of everyone?"

"I will be there to support you, and all will accept you. Then you will find the cure you need, for only an accepted daughter of the Goddess can receive her full gifts and blessings."

"Gifts…Blessings…" Melinda looked to her mother.

"You are a healer, not only with your knowledge and medications, but with your hands and touch. It will appear when you are accepted and I bless you under the full moon. Your touch will heal, but not this illness."

"Then what do we need to cure them?"

"Luna moon flowers."

"But…No one has seen a flower in…"

"Three generations since the last Luna was accepted and loved. You will walk through and around my fire, and the flowers will appear. Gather them in your arms, make an essence from them, and add it to your therapy. This is the secret ingredient for the cure. Your friend, River, will know how to accomplish this. As long as you are accepted and loved, the flowers will grow for you under moonlight. You must also recharge your gifts under my moon, or you will fall into a deep coma."

"I understand…Moon flowers…Oh…"

"Remember my words," the Goddess said as she leaned close and pressed a kiss to Melinda's forehead. "Now awaken. You are needed. My guardians are in trouble."

"Mother, no…" Melinda reached out as the Goddess moved away.

"Awaken, daughter. You are needed," the Goddess said.

Melinda opened her eyes and heard a cell phone ringing. She felt the bed move as Collin's weight shifted.

"Yeah…What? Sweet Goddess, no. I'll bring her there," Collin said and rubbed a hand over Melinda's hip.

"Collin? What's happening?" Melinda sat in bed and knuckled her eyes, alert at the tone of Collin's voice.

"They're crashing. We're losing Grant and Zach. You're needed at the clinic to assist. Get up and get dressed," Collin said.

Both were on full alert as they yanked on pants, shirts, and shoes. Collin grabbed his keys and tossed a black jacket at her.

"Put this on. We'll take my bike," he said as they raced into the garage, and he swung a leg over a sleek black Ducati. He held out a helmet to her.

"I don't…"

"Swing your leg over, put your feet here, and hold on tight to me." Collin tugged her close and pushed the helmet in place. "Now, swing on."

She did as he told her, snuggled close to his ass, and pressed in close. She wrapped her arms around his waist. She tucked her head against his back.

Collin fired up the powerful engine as the door opened. He raced them out in the middle of the early morning and down the street. Neither one cared about waking others with the roar and rumble of the motorcycle. The lives of guardians were in precious trouble.

Within moments, Collin pulled to the bay doors, which led straight into the main treatment room. He helped Melinda out of the helmet and let her race away.

Inside the room, Melinda yanked off the jacket, tossed it aside, and went to where Nathan worked on Grant. "What happened? Talk to me..."

"Laura called it in. His vitals began to drop faster. We're losing him," Nathan said as he pressed compressions on the cat's chest.

"Dark moon, no..." Melinda stared at the monitors, which screamed with the alarms. "Get the paddles and a shot of adrenaline." She took over compressions and ordered the amount needed. "Long needle."

Nathan ran to get what was needed. "Laura! Crash cart!" he shouted to the other nurse.

"Here. Annabelle and I found the damn things," Laura said as she pushed the cart into the treatment center.

"Get it going. Charge to three hundred," Melinda said.

"Charging to three hundred," Laura concurred.

Nathan raced over with the needle, put it on the shelf, picked up the pads, and stuck them in place on the jaguar's chest. "Pads in place."

"Charging...Clear!" Laura said.

Melinda stepped back. "Hit it."

Laura pressed the button to send the charge through the pads. Grant's body lifted with the jolt of energy. The monitors continued to beep with the bad rhythm.

"Charge again. Four hundred. Needle," Melinda said as she held out her hand, and Nathan slapped the covered needle in her palm. She uncapped and raised the needle high over the furry chest. "Come on, Grant, you need to fight with us. A little longer, just fight a little longer," she ordered the cat. She jammed the needle deep into his muscles and chest until she hit the heart and punched the plunger down.

"Charging...Clear!" Laura said.

Melinda pulled out the needle. "Hit it."

Another jolt of energy raced through Grant. The monitors flashed with the energy and settled back into normal rhythm.

"We got him. We got him..." Melinda nodded multiple times and leaned forward, bracing herself on the edge of the gurney.

"Mother Moon, this is some scary shit we're dealing with," Nathan said.

"Moon...Goddess...Moon flowers! Luna moon flowers," Melinda said as she lifted her head and stared at everyone.

"What...What did you say, Mel?" Collin asked as he moved from Luca's bed to her.

"My dream...I dreamt of the Goddess. We need the essence of Luna moon flowers to make the therapy work," she said, turning to stare at Collin.

"Moon flowers...They haven't been seen in generations," Laura said. "Where are we going to get those?"

Collin met Melinda's gaze. "I'll call Alex."

"We can't take Luca through the fire. She'll take him. He's too weak, but...the flowers. There will be a way..." Melinda said.

"We need a Luna jaguar for moon flowers. It's part of the legend...One no one has seen for over three generations, certainly not in this area," Laura said.

"One will be there tomorrow," Melinda said.

Laura's mouth opened as she stared at Melinda. "Oh my...sweet moon, you're the daughter of the Goddess?"

Melinda nodded.

Laura moved to take Melinda's hands and bowed until Melinda's hands touched her face. "Sweet daughter of the Goddess..."

"Unbelievable," Nathan said as he leaned against the gurney.

"It is true, my friend. I saw her other form," Collin said and pulled his cell phone and dialed Alex's number.

"He will not be awake," Melinda said.

"Since he took over the clan, he rarely sleeps." Collin listened as the phone was answered. "Alex, we have a plan...No dance, no ritual except for the acceptance and revelation of a Luna. No, we can't take him through the fire. We'll lose him. We almost lost Grant tonight."

Melinda trembled against Laura's gentle embrace.

"No one will harm you. Not among the Fire clan. We adore the Goddess and all her gifts," Laura said. "Especially now that Alex is in charge."

"I need to remember this for tomorrow. I never shift in front of anyone," Melinda said and waited while Collin spoke with Alex. "Collin, the moon flowers...Tell him about the flowers, and he needs to call River."

"Did you hear Melinda?" Collin said and nodded. "Yes, I know no one has seen them, nor did they see a Luna. The Goddess spoke to her tonight in a dream. They'll work in the therapy. River needs to be ready."

Melinda moved and wrapped an arm around Collin's waist, resting her chin on his biceps. She felt his hand move through her pale hair.

"Yes, we'll have the Goddess with us tomorrow. I don't know about the hunt," Collin said.

"She'll protect us from danger. The Goddess said she'll protect us but didn't tell me how," Melinda said.

"Did you..." Collin nodded again as Alex confirmed. "Okay. We'll get back with you later. No, Grant is stable now. Melinda and the others pulled him back to us. They're keeping an eye on Zach and the others. We'll stay here the rest of the night. Thanks, Alex." Collin closed his phone.

"Did he understand?" Melinda asked.

"A little, but will leave it in your hands. He's sending someone over with fresh coffee and food for everyone."

"Oh good, I could use a pickup." Melinda stretched her arms overhead.

"Same here. Been a long night," Laura said as she settled on a stool near Zach and Grant. "Zach is dipping low, but he hasn't gone into a bad rhythm."

"All depends on how they react," she said as she checked Luca's vitals and found his a little lower. She upped the amount of fluid dripping from the IV bag to help counteract things.

Collin's phone rang, and he answered again. "Collin here...Hey, River..." Collin said and listened to the other jaguar. "Yeah, no, you heard right. The Goddess came to her in a dream tonight. The essence of moon flowers is the key. Can you do it?" He pressed a kiss to Melinda's hair and walked away to let them care for the patients.

Chapter 10

By sunset, all members of the clan except for the patients and a few half-breeds watching them were gathered in the great meadow. The bonfire roared to life and seemed to flame higher than ever before. All waited as their High Alpha moved forward to speak before they shifted to begin an anxious hunt through dangerous woods.

"My family, my clan, we're gathered together on this night, facing a loss of some members to a horrific action caused by rogues. Their leader, the one we know as Robert Thurston, wants power, our clan, our lands, and our special gift from our beloved Goddess of the Moon, Selene. He demands this precious gift be brought to him in exchange for the cure," Alex said, his voice rising above the crowd.

Members of the clan muttered, their voices mingling as they called for justice, revenge, and to give this "gift" to the bastard.

Alex let his powerful energy roll over them to help calm their anger. Then he raised his hands to silence them. "We removed my father from power. All I can say is his brother is a carbon copy of him in attitude and temperament. If we give in to his demands, he'll only go for more until we give in to everything. I know my uncle. Some of you may remember him when he was a part of our clan."

There were murmurs from the older members of the clan.

"Robert Thurston isn't a good cat. He forgets the way of the Goddess. This is why we can't give this gift away. She comes from our Goddess. When her home clan sought to cause her harm, the Goddess Selene sent her to us in her wisdom and kindness, giving us the chance and opportunity to accept this great gift." He stepped aside and waved his hand to the fire, which began to alter with his words.

"Let me present her to all of you. Our gift, a rare and precious Luna jaguar, the daughter of Selene..."

At the introduction, the fire flared blue as the sleek, cream-white cat with faint silver-and-gray rosettes mixed in her fur stepped through the flames. She circled around the Alpha, moved with care to stand next to Alex, and let all take a look upon her elegant length. She flicked her tail once, twice, as silence covered the area. Her ears tilted a little in caution.

"Who...Who is she?" one called out.

Others echoed the question.

"Do we all accept this Luna into our clan? Give our Goddess your consent to accept her daughter in both her cat and her human forms. May I present our wonderful new doctor and Luna, Melinda Hurst," Alex introduced.

At the sound of her name, Melinda shifted and rose to her human height. She shook her head to let pale hair cascade down and curl around her naked body. The top of her head reached his shoulder. The silvery tattoo of the Goddess's symbol, a crescent moon, flower, and paw print, stood out on her lower belly above the hip bone.

"Yes! Yes! We accept. Save us from this evil, daughter of Selene, our Luna Melinda..." others from the crowd called.

As the entire clan accepted her with cheers and calls, a silvery light poured down across the meadow. This time an elegant woman appeared, dressed in silver and midnight blue, her pale hair streaming around her shoulders and sparkling with stars.

"Greetings of the moon, my mother," Melinda said with a bow of her head.

"Greetings of the moon, my dearest daughter. Hmm, must not have my daughter unclothed. You need something more befitting the status of my daughter." Selene tilted to kiss her daughter's forehead. Then she waved a hand and clothed her in a silver robe.

Melinda clutched the opening with one hand between her breasts. "Thank you, Mother."

Selene turned to face the rest of the clan. "Children of the Fire Moon Clan, greetings of the moon," the Goddess said. "I thank you for the welcome and acceptance of my daughter, the Luna jaguar of this generation."

The clan all fell to their knees in respect and awe of the Goddess's appearance. Only the Alpha and Melinda remained standing.

"Greetings and blessings of the moon to you, Goddess Selene," Alex said with a deep, gracious bow to the elegant lady.

"Dear Alpha, I know you worry about your clan. Please, have no fear while in my presence and care. You are under my protection," the Goddess said.

"My lady?" Alex questioned.

"On this dangerous night, until the ones who cause you harm are caught, I gift you with the ability to hold back your cats during the nights of the full moon. None of you will feel the urge to shift and hunt. All will be safe."

"Thank you, Mother Goddess, for protecting our clan," Alex said with another low bow.

"I want no more of my beloved children to be harmed by this evil. I, too, wish for them to be stopped and punished for daring to harm any jaguars. They have turned away from their Goddess and are no longer under my protection or care." Selene waved her hands, and a blanket of moonlight touched every clan member, infusing them with her power. "Now all will remain in human form, except those who wish to shift to help protect the clan on this dangerous night. Their cats will respond when needed. I will not leave your guardians helpless in the face of danger. No others will be overwhelmed by the pull of the moon."

When all the cats were calm of their need to shift and hunt under the full moon, Selene turned to her daughter and held out a hand. "Daughter of mine…"

Melinda stepped forward and took her mother's hand in hers.

Selene pressed her lips to Melinda's forehead as more moonlight, brighter than before, surrounded them, gifting the young Luna with powers. She leaned back to reveal a crescent moon mark upon Melinda's forehead. Before their eyes, the mark disappeared as her hands glowed with the same light.

"The gift of healing is within your hands and body, but be wise and cautious with this power. You cannot bring one who is dead back. One near death or extremely injured will tax your gift and strength. Too much healing and it will weaken your entire body. When you feel weak of mind and body, you must sleep under the light of the moon to recharge your gifts and strength," Selene cautioned her daughter.

"Yes, Mother, I understand. Thank you for this gift to heal my clan. What of the illness plaguing our clan?" Melinda said.

"The illness is not natural but caused by a toxin. You cannot heal their illnesses until the foreign toxin is removed from their bodies. It is the same for all unnatural illnesses or injuries. Please take care with your gift, or it could rebound upon you."

"I understand."

Selene smiled, turned, and held a hand toward Collin. "Come forward, chosen mate of my daughter."

Collin swallowed when he was addressed by the Goddess and moved in a quiet, graceful fashion. He knelt on one knee before her, lowering his head in respect. "Greetings of the moon to you, Goddess Selene."

"Greetings of the moon to you, Collin. Strong and noble mate of my daughter, one of two chosen by Fate and Destiny, you are wise and capable beyond your years, yet filled with an impish quality to counteract times of despair and dispel the feelings of anger within others. Yes, you are a wise choice for my daughter," the Goddess intoned as she rested a hand on his head. "You were the first to accept my daughter without fear or greed in the woods. Even when you looked upon her true form, you did not try to harm her."

"No, my lady, I felt only adoration toward her," Collin answered.

"This feeling will turn to love for you and your mate, Luca."

"I thank you, my Goddess." Collin lifted his head under her touch at the sound of his mate's name on her lips. "We fear for his life and the others. We don't want to see them pass from this evil poison. It's no way for a proud jaguar to leave this earth."

"They will be returned to you. Daughter of mine, take your mate's hand in yours," the Goddess said. "Rise, mate of my daughter."

Collin rose to his full height and felt Melinda's soft hand curl against his.

"Fire Moon Clan, beloved of the Goddess, I gift to you another powerful triad to help guide your clan to the future. I bless them as I blessed the previous triad who stepped through my fire. No dance is needed, for they are now mated before my eyes, along with their third mate, who lies apart, but his soul is with them." The Goddess covered their joined hands with hers, and moonlight filled the space between them once more.

Both Collin and Melinda hissed as the ancient markings of a Goddess-blessed mating appeared on their left biceps. With a henna-like appearance, the swirls and designs of the cuff tattoo mark were unique to them, this one filled with a crescent moon, paw, and a flower to show they were mated to a Luna daughter.

"Now, my daughter and your chosen will walk through and around the fires to call forth the first of the mystical Luna moon flowers to grow and blossom. Daughter, show your mate how to make the flowers blossom among the flames."

With joined hands, Melinda led Collin to the blue bonfire. As she saw in her dreams, she wove them through the flames and around the pit almost as if they were performing the mating dance. After they passed, green sprouts rose from the ground. When they reached the side of the Goddess, the sprouts turned to full flowers with brilliant white blossoms.

"Behold! The first Luna moon flowers of the Fire Moon Clan. They are both a gift and a cure. Only my daughter and her chosen mates may grow and gather the flowers from the ground. Once plucked, you have until morning to do with them as you wish for their most potent of gifts. Touched by sunlight, they will wilt and disappear, for they can only grow and flourish under the moonlight."

Melinda squeezed Collin's hand as they studied the beautiful blossoms, the way to save Luca and the other stricken cats.

"Mate of my daughter, you will find your home somewhat altered," the Goddess said with a smile.

"Altered, my lady?"

"I had an arboretum added to your home while we stand here. Grown from the ground and covered with glass. My daughter will sleep there under the moonlight to help concentrate and strengthen her gifts after use. Plus, she may coax the flowers to grow in the beds I created under the moon as needed."

"Thank you, my lady, for securing all this for your daughter," Collin said.

"Protect and love her as well as this arboretum, for it is vital for her health and life," Selene said.

"I promise I will protect and guard both with my life," Collin promised, pressing a hand to his chest and bowing his head.

"Gather the flowers. Create the essence vital to save our cats." Selene lifted her hand to Melinda's cheek. "Daughter of mine, here is the garden of evil you all must seek and destroy." She sent the images of the garden and its location.

"Thank you for showing me the way to the garden, Mother. I'll make sure of its destruction and those who create this vial poison. No other cat will be harmed by its evil," Melinda said with a nod of understanding.

"Until our next meeting, daughter, take care of yourself and our blessed clan." Selene looked upon the clan, drifting back to the moonlight and blue fire, and dissipated from sight in a blur of starlight sparkles.

"Are you all right?" Melinda whispered to Collin, who stood a little starstruck.

"Umm. Mother? The Goddess is your mother," Collin said as he swallowed hard. He stared at her.

Melinda smiled and nodded. "She is." She cupped a hand to his cheek. "Are you all right with this?"

"I have you as my Goddess-blessed mate, along with Luca. I want nothing more."

"Other than to have Luca standing here with us."

Collin nodded in agreement. "He will never believe we spoke with the Goddess."

"I don't think it will be her last visit. She'll want to meet him, too." Melinda grinned. "The flowers…We must gather the flowers and heal him and the others."

Melinda and Collin moved to gather and pluck all the flowers from the ground. She motioned to River, who stepped forward with a large basket, and they poured the precious blossoms inside.

"Hurry, River. As the Goddess mentioned, you have a limited time to create the essence this evening. Once you're sure of the therapy mixture, bring everything you need to the clinic. We're losing ground against this poison," Melinda urged the other cat. She couldn't believe the amount of flowers they saw inside the basket. She knew these beautiful petals would save everyone.

River hugged the full basket close to his body, protecting the Goddess-given gift with his life. "I'll not let you down."

"I know. Hurry."

"River, this way. I'll get you back to the lab," the powerful Gideon said as he moved forward.

"I'll do everything I can to create this cure," River said and left with Gideon at his side.

Melinda lifted her gaze to her new mate. "As much I wish to return home to complete our mating, I don't feel it is right."

"Not without Luca at our side. I know," Collin said as he caressed her cheek with his fingers. "I feel the same."

Melinda kissed him, tender and sweet, but held back the passion. She touched his face with her fingers as she studied his gaze and kissed him once more. "Let's return to the clinic, then, sit by our mate, and hope River can create the bit of magic we need… No… Wait. We have one more thing to do tonight."

"What else is there to do?"

"The garden. We must find the garden and destroy it."

"The moon and the danger—we can't go out in this," Collin said.

"They're under the same thrall of power, but unlike us they'll be helpless to the pull. The rogues must shift tonight, but we don't feel the compulsion, thanks to the Goddess. We can hunt down the garden and destroy it with fire while they hunt."

"They could still have their claws dipped in the poison."

"They could, but I doubt it since they're hunting a different prey tonight, not us."

"May I offer my congratulations on your mating, Collin, Melinda." Alex moved closer and stood next to them.

"Thank you, but there is no congratulations until our third is with us," Collin said.

"Of course," Alex said with a low nod of his head. "As for the hunt, your lovely mate is correct. They'll have to go out and hunt someone other than us. It's far past time we took a turn at them."

"We can't go in alone," Collin said.

"Who said anything about alone? You're part of a clan, and all of us want a piece of the damn rogues," Alex said as he rolled his shoulders.

Other guardians stepped forward, including Sebastian and Raphael, part of the first triad and more powerful because of their unique mating.

"As if I would let all of you hunt alone," another male called out. His voice was midnight deep and powerful.

They all turned to find a tall, golden-haired man walk toward them out of nowhere. A long black trench coat swirled around him. A walking stick held in one hand.

"Xavier…" Alex said in a soft voice.

"Alex, how are you? Haven't called me for some time," the stranger said with a slow smile.

"Who…" Melinda whispered to Collin, stepping closer to him.

The golden stranger turned and bowed low to her. "Lady Luna, I presume, it's a sincere honor to meet you. I am Xavier, the humble owner of Twilight, the club on the other side of the valley."

Melinda felt the power swirling around the man…the vampire. "I didn't think your kind existed."

"Our numbers are few, but we're still here. We're surviving," Xavier said. "I help to protect this clan and encase it with some…magical measures."

"Magic?"

"What is given to vampires, yes. We can discuss more about it another time, perhaps? Now we need to deal with some rogues. Shall we go?" Xavier waved a hand toward the forest.

"Time to hunt some rogues," Sebastian agreed with a lethal grin.

"No, we go after the garden first. If rogues are on watch, kill them. Otherwise, our main focus is the garden," Alex said with a sideways glance at Xavier, and then he turned to their Luna for confirmation.

Melinda nodded. "The garden is our first order of business. Without it, they can't create more of the poison. If we find their stock, we'll destroy it as well."

"Time to shift and hunt our enemies," Raphael said, his voice holding a touch of Spanish flavor and tone.

"I require half of the guardians to join us on our hunt to destroy the garden," Alex said as he called over the gathering. "The rest must stay behind to protect our clan and homes. Who will join us?"

Raucous cheers shouted as guardians moved through the crowds and gathered around them.

"Then call forth your cats, and let's go hunting!" Alex said with a burst of his power over those gathered.

Chapter 11

With Xavier and Alex on one side and Collin protecting her other, Melinda led the large group of jaguars through the forest and toward the climb over the valley. She followed the map and directions given to her by the Goddess as she jumped over rocks and fallen trees. She chuffed toward one side where there were caves. She knew there were some rogues living within those caves.

Some guardians moved to the caves on quiet pads, not a branch or rock disturbed under their massive paws. They sniffed and searched the openings for any fresh scents, but returned to show there was no one at home.

Melinda turned a different branch on an unmarked patch as others spread out behind her to cover more ground. They dipped down and then went over another crest, where she crouched down on her paws. The others quickly followed her. The vampire was a dark flash racing along with them.

Down in the small valley below, a large group of jaguars gathered, shifting under the moonlight and fighting with others. Snarls and yelps echoed around them from the multiple tangles of cats.

Finally, one large golden jaguar stepped toward the gathering. He swatted a pair of tussling jaguars and snarled at them. He moved to bite another cat's shoulder and tossed him out of the fighting. He screamed to alert everyone to his presence. When he got their attention, he leapt off to one side and led his group on a hunt. Only four jaguars remained behind, gathered around a small cottage.

Collin licked her ear to comfort her after the vicious scene below. He motioned for half of the guardians to go around the far side of the clearing to keep an eye on the hunting jaguars. Before he could send guardians down to deal with the ones left behind, the vampire held a hand to stop them.

"I will handle them. You concentrate on the rest," Xavier said.

Collin growled, and five black jaguars stepped forward to accompany Xavier.

Xavier looked over them and nodded. With ease, Xavier and the five jaguars disappeared into the night, camouflaged against the rocks, trees, and ground.

Without warning or a fight, the four jaguar rogues were dragged back into the tree line and disposed of with no sound echoing across the valley. An exhale whispered up to them as notice all was done.

Collin nudged Melinda to move into the valley. While he left several others behind to cover their exit or alert to danger, he accompanied Melinda down with Alex on her other side. He was glad to scent Sebastian and Raphael near him, two of their finest guardians. While this wasn't much of a fight with the rogues, no one was taking chances. Not with their precious Luna in the mix.

Xavier stepped out of the forest, wiped a piece of cloth along a thin blade, and tossed it to the ground. He slid the blade back into the walking stick. "All is clear, my lady. The others are dealing with the bodies."

Melinda lifted her nose, scented the air, and padded to the small cabin. She went around to the back and skidded to a stop. She shifted back to her human form and nodded to Xavier for his quiet, deadly work, but her hands lifted to cover her mouth.

"Darling, what is it?" Collin asked as he shifted with her, wrapping his arms around her waist.

"Look at it…" she whispered as they stared over the acre-plus garden of pure, utter evil.

"There is more inside the cabin. This is where they were making the crap. What do you wish to do with all this, Luna?" Sebastian said as he shifted with his partner and exited the cabin.

"Burn it. Burn everything," she said, her hands dropping to fists at her sides.

Sebastian looked to Alex, who nodded in agreement. "As you wish." He returned to the cabin.

"Have everyone spread out and claw up the garden. Urinate on the soil. Ruin everything. Pile everything to be burned," Melinda instructed to Alex, who remained in jaguar form.

Alex called to the others and moved to the garden. Taking a spot, he started to drag his claws in deep, ripping plants out of the ground down to their roots before pausing to take a piss and mix it into the soil.

"Hmm. Don't know if I enjoy this pleasant side of your nature, Alexander," Xavier said in a wry tone.

Alex chuffed at the vampire and went on to another section. Soon, all the other jaguars followed him in various sections.

"Felines," Xavier said and shook his head. He went to the cabin to assist Sebastian and Raphael.

Melinda pressed against Collin, who held her tight. "This could have killed everyone in the clan. If they shot one of those darts into a cub, they wouldn't have survived."

"We're getting rid of everything. They'll have to start over from nothing."

"I want Thurston under my claws."

"You'll get the chance, but not tonight." Collin leaned over and nuzzled her cheek with his to soothe her anger. "We must concentrate on the garden and getting our mate and the others healed. There will be another time when we can make him pay for his crimes."

"I wish Luca was here with us to watch this. He fought for it."

"He'll be by our side soon."

"Luna Melinda, we found some…volatile chemicals and created a few batches. Everything will be in ashes when we leave," Sebastian said as Raphael lifted a few beakers.

"I love playing with this stuff," Raphael said with a grin.

"That's putting your attraction to volatile things in a mild fashion," Xavier said as he leaned against the doorframe.

"Oh shoo, fang one," Raphael said. "You're upset you didn't think of it first."

"Fang one?" Xavier asked in a mild, dangerous tone.

"Enough… What do we do with these chemicals?" Melinda said as she stepped forward.

"Sorry, Luna. Simple. Just throw them on the pile and toss a match, which we happen to have." Raphael lifted a box and rattled it. "Boom."

"And the cabin?" Melinda asked.

"We placed several batches around the interior. All we need is to light the fuse," Raphael said.

"We'll wait until the garden is destroyed, set the flames, and race away before they can see the sky lit up with the fire. Though Thurston will not be killed in the process, he would have nothing left when he returns. For now this option will work," she said. "Do it."

"With pleasure, my Luna," Raphael said with a deep bow, rather comical in his nudity.

"Your lady mate is very lucky to have the both of you," Melinda told them.

"On the fair side, I helped things along," Xavier pointed out as he stepped away from the cabin and placed a hand on Sebastian's shoulder.

Sebastian tilted his head to the side and looked up at the vampire. "How do you think that?"

"I helped her see the beauty in herself," Xavier said. "As I do with all who come to my club seeking help, guidance, or assistance."

"And you know we always adore you for it," Sebastian said.

Xavier grinned, squeezed Sebastian's shoulder, and moved away from them. He swirled the black coat around his height before he disappeared from their sight.

"What the…Where did he go?" Melinda looked around.

"Back to his club, I presume. Vampires and fire don't get along with one another. I noticed he's been…different," Sebastian said with a glance to Raphael.

"Hmm, I noticed it, too. Very odd for him to be withdrawn from the clan," Raphael agreed. He looked to Melinda and smiled. "As for our beloved mate, we love her dearly, along with our soon-to-be cubs." His Spanish accent deepened with his obvious love and adoration for their mate.

"She's only pissed she's not here to help," Sebastian said with a chuckle.

"In her current state, no, I wouldn't want her to be here. Best those cubs stay inside her for a few more weeks," Melinda said.

Both soon-to-be fathers groaned.

Collin chuckled and patted both of them on their shoulders. "Hang in there. It's almost over, boys. Then you'll have no sleep, crying cubs, and a hormonal mate."

"Oh, thank you so much," Raphael said.

"Really?" Sebastian asked as he shoved Collin back. "Wait until it's your turn."

"I can only wish and hope," Collin said as he glanced at his mate.

"Don't look at me," Melinda said and heard all three men chuckle.

Alex returned to their side after sniffing the area where Xavier disappeared, and he sat with a chuff.

"Thank you, Alpha and guardians," Melinda said and turned to Raphael and Sebastian. "Light everything up."

"Would you care for the first toss at the pile?" Raphael held out one of the beakers.

"Please." She took the beaker and threw it hard at the enormous pile of torn plants and roots. She heard the glass smash.

Collin threw a few more at the pile. Alex shifted, hefted a beaker in one hand, glared at the enormous pile, and then tossed it hard. Other guardians did the same, all wanting a piece of the destruction.

Sebastian gathered a few sticks covered in the mixed chemicals and held them for Raphael to light them with the matches. The branches immediately caught fire. Sebastian passed a branch to Melinda, Collin, and Alex and waved a hand to the pile.

"Do the honors, Luna. Raphael and I will cover the cabin. Everyone else should race back to the forest where the rest wait. We don't want to be here when the flames spark the chemicals," Sebastian said.

"Yeah. Big boom!" Raphael said with a chuckle.

"How did we not know of your tendencies to play with dangerous chemicals and explosives?" Alex asked.

"Don't really need them, but I like to play around."

"Until you nearly blew up the house and I forbid any more playing inside," Sebastian added.

"Blew up the house? Now, I wouldn't go that far," Raphael said as everyone around them lifted their eyebrows to their hairlines. "What? Wrong chemical mix. It was just a little smoke."

Sebastian snorted. "We needed to repair the entire floor from the little bit of smoke."

"Oops?"

Sebastian groaned.

"We'll continue this back in our valley. Melinda, the fire," Alex said.

"With pleasure, Alpha," Melinda said and threw the stick end over end, the flames eating the branch. When it landed, a brilliant fire whooshed over one side.

"Time to start backing away," Raphael warned as Collin and Alex tossed their sticks toward the massive pile.

After watching the pile burn, Melinda shifted with Collin and Alex and raced away. The last to leave was Raphael, who dropped several fire sticks on the cabin, which took to flames. He shifted to his black jaguar and ran.

Before they made it to the top of the hill, the pile and cabin sent off huge booms as flames roared over them. All the cats looked at Raphael, who gave them a kitty grin.

Alex and Collin shook their heads as Sebastian cuffed his mate with one paw.

A high-pitched cry sounded from the area when another secondary boom shuddered through the forest, blowing the cabin to smithereens. Melinda stepped forward as if she would flee back down the hill to rescue the one who screamed. Collin leapt in front of her and growled. She transformed back to her human self along with Collin, who placed his hands on her shoulders.

"Someone was down there. Someone is hurt because of my decision," she cried out.

"They're part of the rogues and deserved the death. You can't risk your life to help them, no matter your oath as a doctor," Collin argued.

Tears of frustration and need filled her eyes as Melinda stared at the burning cabin and then to her mate.

"Please, my love, we need to return to save our mate. Let this place burn," Collin said, cupping her cheek with one hand.

At the reminder of their mate lying in the clinic, waiting for them to heal him, Melinda nodded, nuzzled Collin's hand, and stepped back. She changed back to her jaguar and turned away from the fire.

Collin transformed, padded next to her side, and nuzzled her flank with his muzzle. He chuffed and she answered.

While the sky filled with the brilliant colors of chemically induced flames that destroyed all dangers, they ran through the forest. Melinda, Collin, and Nathan headed to the clinic. Nathan nosed open the door for the others to precede him inside before they shifted.

"Welcome back. I hope you were successful," Laura said as she held out three robes for them.

"The garden and cabin are destroyed. It was massive," Melinda said.

"What about Thurston? Is he dead?"

"No. Thurston ran with the rest of his followers under the moon, but we'll return to deal with him. He's not getting away with these vicious crimes to our clan," Melinda said as she slipped her arms into the robe. "I need to change. Did Gideon and River return with the moon flowers and infusion?"

"Gideon called, and they're on their way," Laura said.

"Good. Good."

"Fresh scrubs or sweats, along with various shoes, are in the laundry room. Different sizes are on the shelves, all organized. We've had a lot of helpers this evening since they didn't need to shift, but wanted to keep busy. All the upstairs work is completed and ready for patients."

"This place is becoming a real clinic." Melinda led the others to the laundry room. She snagged a pair of scrubs, plain lingerie, socks, and Crocs. She went to her office with Collin, who grabbed sweats and Crocs.

"The infusion will work, Mel," Collin reassured her after they dressed. He tugged her into his arms and placed their lips together. "My mate. My beautiful mate." He lifted a hand and traced her henna marking.

Melinda raised her gaze to meet his while her fingers touched his cheek.

"This will work and you need to believe in your mother and River's work," Collin insisted when he noticed the fear and apprehension mixed within her expression.

She startled when someone knocked on their door.

"Doc Melinda? River is here," Laura called out.

"We'll be right there." Melinda twisted her hair up in a bun, found a band to secure it, and shook out her hands when her fingers trembled.

"It'll work," Collin repeated, sensing she needed to hear the words again. He grasped her hands in his and kissed both of them. "You'll bring all of them back to us."

"I hope you're right," she whispered.

Chapter 12

Stepping into the treatment room filled with the stricken jaguars, Melinda watched River lift the chelation properties from a plastic tub and place them on the nearby table. She saw Nathan bring over several IV bags to fill with the treatment.

"I thank you for hurrying, River. How did the process go?" She washed her hands and gloved them. She stood next to them and stared at the various jugs filled with an almost pearlescent liquid.

"Quite easy and I was amazed. I crushed the flowers and stems, filtered them for the liquid essence as they broke down, and combined everything. We need to transfer the chelation into IV bags," River said.

"Will it work?"

"We'll find out." River pulled out several large syringes and tubing. "The best way I know to fill the bags."

Nathan opened and turned all the bags upside down. "Bags are ready."

"Good." River clamped the syringe, backflow valves, and tubing together. "Okay. Fill the syringes with the fluid." He placed the tubing in one of the jugs and began to draw back on the syringe, drawing the liquid up the tube, and tapped it for any air. He pulled off the tube, placed the end of the syringe in the nearest IV bag, and pushed the stopper. "We'll need several draws for each bag."

Melinda and Nathan repeated the process that River showed them. Once they had multiple bags filled, Melinda clamped and secured the bag stems. She hooked a bag per jaguar, connected everything, and started the drip. She turned off the other treatments.

"How much will we need per jaguar?" she asked River.

"I'm not sure. Maybe two bags, perhaps three. It depends on the amount of toxin and damage inside them," he said.

"I'll start them on the first bag and we'll check them throughout the night. This is going to be one long watch." She picked up her stethoscope and went to Luca's side. She found Collin sitting next to him, one hand on Luca's wide paw. "Now is where we learn if this works."

"It'll work," Collin said.

Placing the pieces in her ears, Melinda moved the stethoscope over Luca's chest, listening to his heart and even breathing. "He's steady and strong."

"He's tough, wouldn't give up the fight." Collin caressed one of Luca's soft ears.

Melinda kissed Collin and then Luca's furry cheek, and moved to where Grant and Zacharias rested. She was worried about the fluctuations in Grant's vitals. "Come on, Grant, keep fighting. We found a cure."

When she moved to the younger victims, Bree Anne and Parker, she gave a comforting smile to Bree Anne's parents, who stood guard. She listened to them and slung the scope around her neck. "They're both holding their own. It's a matter of time under the chelation until the moon flowers get into their systems and help clear things out."

"Any side effects to expect?" Dawson asked.

"Perhaps some vomiting, exhaustion, a fever, and, I hope, a shift back to human form. I'm hoping the moon flower essence helps support them through this since it's grown for jaguars. I've read about its medicinal properties."

"Then it's wonderful to have a true Luna among our clan who can bring forth these magical flowers," Juliet said as she reached out and grasped Melinda's wrist. "You're doing a fabulous job of caring for everyone."

"Thank you, Juliet. All I can say is give this treatment time."

When both parents nodded to the simple request, Melinda headed to the second treatment room, where she checked on the rest of her patients. Six more guardians arrived wounded within the last two days. After noting all of their files with the latest stats and chelation amounts, she returned to Luca's side.

"Come, take a rest." Collin tugged her down on his lap after she removed the gloves.

Melinda sat across his lap and nuzzled her head against his chest and shoulders.

The hours passed and things were quiet. Alex and some more guardians stopped at the clinic, brought food and coffee to keep them going, and learned how things were progressing with the treatment. Other than changing everyone's IV bag with a second one, there wasn't much change.

"Perhaps I processed the moon flowers incorrectly. Perhaps I didn't use enough of the essence in the chelation." River paced, dragging hands through his hair.

"Would you sit and relax? You did everything correct. Give the treatment time." Gideon wrapped a long arm around River's waist, lifted him off his feet, and plopped his ass on the nearest stool. "Stay." He pointed a finger into River's chest.

The other cat blinked and gazed upon him. "Yes, sir," he said in a meek tone.

Crossing arms over his chest, Gideon moved back to his place against the wall. "I watched every step of your process, River. No one else would have figured those difficult calculations and procedures. Besides, it's been generations since anyone has worked with moon flowers."

"I know... Still, perhaps I should have used more essence in the chelation."

"Stop second-guessing yourself. You'll drive yourself nuts, and I'm not watching it happen." Gideon raised an eyebrow.

"Okay. I understand," River said then muttered so everyone still heard him. "Slave driver."

"No, you do enough to push yourself. I try to get you to slack off now and then," Gideon pointed out as he dropped a hand to muss River's hair with tenderness and care.

Melinda snickered against Collin's chest. "Looks like there is someone interested in one another," she whispered.

"Hmm. I wouldn't have thought of them as a couple. Still, Gideon volunteered to take care of River first back at your old place," Collin said.

"Perhaps he had a crush and finally acted on it. I believe Gideon will pull River out of his lab a little more often and protect him. I think they'll be good for one another."

"I hope so. We need something good to come out of this mess." Collin moved and pressed his lips to her temple.

A soft sound murmured through the room. Melinda sat away from Collin and studied her patients.

"What…"

Melinda pressed her fingers to Collin's mouth. She lowered her gaze to Luca and saw his eyelids fluttering. "Luca…" She moved off Collin's lap and stood over Luca. "Come on, Luca, come back to us."

Luca moaned as if in pain, his paws curled and flexed, before his body rippled and shifted back. A naked Luca lay on his side on the gurney, his head turned a little.

"Luca…you're back!"

Trusting in her mother's gift, Melinda placed her hands on Luca and called forth the healing light. Somehow she could feel and see everything inside him. She could no longer feel the toxins. She pushed to finish healing him and gave him a bit of energy to come out of the light coma. As her hands darkened, Luca opened his eyes and blinked.

"Luca!" Collin wrapped an arm around Melinda to steady her and placed his other hand on Luca's head. His fingers drifted through the silky hair.

Luca blinked, moved his mouth as if trying to talk, and closed his eyes.

"Water. Get him a glass of water with a straw," Melinda said.

"On it!" Nathan rushed out and returned with a small glass and straw. He grabbed a light blanket and spread it over Luca's body.

"Thanks, Nathan and check the others." Melinda took the cup and held the straw to Luca's lips. "Small sips, Luca, take a little water."

Luca opened his eyes, saw the straw, and wrapped his lips around the end. He drew a few sips, licked his lips, and rolled to his back. A moan escaped as a few things creaked and protested.

Melinda and Collin spotted the henna mate band on Luca's left arm. She touched the marking with her fingers, so pleased to see it there, and hoped Luca didn't hate how he was mated without his knowledge.

"Hi...What'd I miss?" Luca asked with a rough, scratchy voice. It was soft and low from disuse.

"Hi, Luca. Sweet moon, it's damn good to have you back." Collin chuckled. "A lot, my friend. You missed too much."

"How are you feeling?" Melinda asked.

"Like I haven't moved in days, and still furry, but better," Luca said.

"What do you remember?"

"Passing out at your clinic from the pain and whatever they shot me with."

"It was a created toxin, a poison that trapped you in your jaguar form along with all the others. River found the correct therapy to clear the toxin. You're the first to wake." Melinda leaned over and kissed Luca on his forehead. "I'm so happy you're back."

"Me, too, partner," Collin said, giving Luca a full kiss on the lips. "I missed you."

"Doc Melinda! Zacharias and Grant are waking up. They shifted back to human," Nathan called out.

Melinda looked up at Nathan's call and back to Luca.

"Go. I'm not going anywhere," Luca said.

Melinda captured his lips in a soft kiss. "Keep giving him some water and help stretch his limbs for blood flow," she told Collin and moved away.

"We'll be fine," Luca said.

Collin rubbed his hand over Luca's chest.

Melinda went to Grant first, worried about him after his medical crisis. Instead of the black jaguar, she looked down upon a six-one physically fit body topped with ebony hair and finished with midnight-blue eyes, which moved to find her. He sipped from the straw from the cup of water Nathan had got for them.

"Hello, Grant and welcome back. You gave us a few scares," she said as she let one of her hands glow over his chest as she searched.

"Hi, Doc. Wow. You glow," Grant said with a lopsided smile.

"A gift our Goddess gave me tonight."

"I heard. Nathan was catching us up."

"Yeah, a lot happened while you were taking a catnap. How do you feel?"

"Better. What the hell did they knock us out with? I couldn't control my cat."

"A horrible concoction created from toxic plants and heavy metals. We destroyed everything, though, so they can't create more."

"Didn't think it would hit so bad, but man… After the fight, I was gone. So was Zach."

"It was fast acting to drop you, but we got the antidote, thanks to River."

"Ahh…Good on the professor." Grant let out a yawn and stretched his arms.

"Take a nap. Sleep will help you heal, and I want the IV to finish. Then we'll transfer all of you to separate rooms upstairs."

"Upstairs?"

"Yeah, we have a full clinic now." She patted him on the chest and moved to Zacharias's gurney. She noticed that his feet dangled over the edge, thanks to his six-five frame. "I need to order longer gurneys for you big guys. Sorry about that. We were rushing to get supplies when all of you were hurt."

"I'm used to it, Doc. Not the first time my feet dangled," Zacharias said.

She glanced over his careless chestnut hair, which flopped over his face and shoulders and those gleaming scotch-amber eyes. She would have looked at him as a potential mate if she wasn't mated.

"How are we all doing?" Zach asked.

"The therapy is working, finally, and all of you should be awake and back in human forms before dawn. We didn't lose anyone."

"How many guardians got hit?"

"Nine guardians total. This includes you, Grant, and Luca. Also, two teens got hit when they snuck out to a cabin for some fun."

"Teens?"

"Hmm. Bree Anne Essex and her boyfriend, Parker."

"Sweet dark moon. No one else?"

Melinda shook her head, amazed at his concern for everyone else before his health. She gave him a boost with her healing energy. "They had a big enough garden to destroy the clan."

"Is it gone?"

"We destroyed it and the cabin where they made everything tonight. It seems Raphael likes to play with chemicals and things that go boom.

Zacharias let out a gruff laugh. "Yeah. He's fond of them, unfortunately for Sebastian and Hillary. She is well? Her..."

"They're fine, all of them. I will be keeping a close eye on her and her unborn cubs."

Zacharias let out a long sigh and closed his eyes.

"Sleep, Zacharias. It'll help you heal." She patted his broad chest.

"Thank you," he whispered.

"You're welcome." Melinda watched him drift into a light sleep, noticing River and Gideon walking closer to watch over the pair of guardians. She pressed a hand on River's forearm. "You did it. It's working."

"We both did it," River said as he covered her hand. "We're healing them."

"This means you're a part of the clinic now. I got the space for another doctor."

River chuckled. "Nah, I prefer my small lab."

"Whatever you wish, but know you have a place here." Popping a kiss on his cheek, Melinda went to the teenagers who returned to human form while she spoke with Zacharias. She glanced at Nathan. "Is he always like that? Concerned for others before himself?"

Nathan nodded. "All the time. It's why everyone loves him."

"I can tell. He's a good cat and a strong guardian." She glanced at the two teens. "Hello, you two. Welcome back. I'm Doctor Melinda Hurst."

After checking everyone in both rooms, pleased all returned to human form, Melinda dragged a hand through her hair as she returned to Luca and Collin.

"Everyone is good?" Collin asked as he dragged her back on his lap.

"Yeah. Everyone is healed."

"Perhaps you can tell me how I got a mating mark? I don't remember our dance. At least I hope the dance was with the both of you," Luca said with a wry grin.

"Yeah, about the mark…" Collin glanced to Melinda, who snickered. He pulled up his sleeve to reveal his mark.

At the same time, Melinda dropped her coat down to reveal an identical mark. "You're mated to us. There was no dance."

Luca lifted an eyebrow. "No dance? Then how…"

"My mother blessed our mating after removing the urge to shift since everyone feared the danger of running in the forest with those rogues."

"Your mother?"

"The Goddess Selene," Melinda said. "As I mentioned before, I'm a Luna jaguar, a true daughter of Selene. I was given to a clan who didn't accept me. They betrayed her gift to them. Tonight everyone in the Fire Moon Clan accepted me."

"As is proper of a true Goddess of the moon-worshipping clan," Collin added. "Luca, she appeared to all of us!"

"Who? Melinda?" Luca asked, confused.

"No, the Goddess Selene. She walked out of the fire and moonlight and took form. She spoke with Alex and me, along with Melinda and the clan. We all could see her."

"Are you kidding me?"

"Truth, buddy."

Luca looked to Melinda. "You're a real Luna? I kept thinking it was a myth."

Melinda pulled in her lower lip to nibble on it. "You're not afraid of being mated to a Luna, are you?"

"Hell, no and I love you no matter what your color is. Though, it would be odd to have blue kittens."

Melinda chuckled and leaned over to capture Luca's lips. "Thank you," she whispered against his lips. "No chance of blue kittens, but maybe a couple of white ones."

"They'll be gorgeous like their momma. One more thing you need to clarify, please. I wasn't losing it when I saw your hands glow. Right?"

"No, you're not going crazy. It's another gift from my mother. We can also grow moon flowers."

"Moon flowers? They're real."

"They're what helped to heal you. River pulled the essence from the flowers and incorporated it into the chelation."

Luca turned his head to look for River. "Damn. Sweet dark moon, thank you, River, for everything."

River lifted his head, gave a shy smile, and nodded. "I didn't do much, but you're welcome. All of you."

"You did more than enough. I couldn't have saved them without your help and knowledge, River." Melinda returned her attention to Luca.

"So, how did we get this here mark without the dance?" Luca asked as he touched the henna marking.

"Since you were sick and couldn't enter the fire, the Goddess gave us her blessing and mark without dancing. She knew I was Melinda's mate," Collin said.

"She touched our joined hands and covered us in moonlight as she blessed us along with you. Then we felt the henna markings form," Melinda said. "Forgive us for accepting the mating without you by our side."

"There is nothing to forgive, my dearest one. As long as I'm part of the consummation of our mating," Luca said with a raised eyebrow.

"Things have been a little busy around here to think about lovemaking, let alone to get her in bed," Collin said.

Melinda smacked his arm. "What he means is that Collin and I haven't finished the mating. We wanted you with us. Neither of us felt it was right to fall into bed unless you were awake."

Luca lifted her hand and kissed her knuckles before resting their hands on his chest. He then did the same with Collin's hand.

"You can't get rid of us," Collin said as he leaned over and kissed Luca's forehead.

"Not going to bother to try," Luca said.

A knock on the double doors pulled Melinda's attention. She saw Alex in the doorway and waved him inside. "I need to speak with the Alpha. Try to get some rest so we can take you home."

Luca chuckled and closed his eyes.

Melinda kissed Collin's cheek and left to go to Alex. She watched him as he looked around with pure awe at all the patients awake and talking.

"You performed a miracle here," he said in a soft tone.

"River made it happen," Melinda said as she waved River over. "He created the chelation and found a way to make the moon flower essence. This is his cure."

"Again, both of us created this cure. We wouldn't have moon flowers if it wasn't for you," River said as he shook hands with Alex.

"Either way…Both of you, thank you from the bottom of my heart for saving our clan members. Without either one of you here, I don't know what we would have done. We would have lost them," Alex said, pressing a hand to his chest and bowing in respect.

Melinda glanced at River, who blushed at the high praise, and squeezed his hand. "Thank you, Alpha."

"When will they be able to go home?"

"Depends on how they recover, and I want to make sure this last IV finishes. We'll roll them into separate rooms upstairs so they can further heal and rest. I suspect within the next two days, most will go home, perhaps sooner."

"I know you hope for sooner with Luca," Alex said with a wink.

Melinda chuckled and flushed.

"I understand you haven't finished moving your things. Is there anything you need help with? I can request some guardians and their mates to assist you. I'm sure Luca will also wish to move his things from the guardians' complex."

"I'll need to speak with Luca and Collin before making a decision."

"Of course and either way, let me know."

"Thank you, Alpha—"

"Alex. Please, I'm Alex among friends," Alex said. "I'm Alpha in formal gatherings."

"Alex, then," Melinda said.

"I'll let you return to your duties. I hope I can move around and speak with the patients."

"Could you wash and dry your hands with the antiseptic wash? I don't want any possible contaminates to move around."

"I understand. I was digging in that horrible garden and washed up at home, but you have stronger soap here."

"Exactly," Melinda said.

"Go on. I know what to do," Alex said and went to the sink.

Melinda returned to Luca and Collin. She settled down for another long vigil.

Chapter 13

As Melinda predicted, all of the stricken jaguars were up and moving around by the second day. Their normal fast healing pace kicked in once all the toxin was destroyed by the moon flower chelation. She sent them all home with best wishes in between other patients, who came and went now that the clinic was open full time.

Melinda performed so many wellness checks on cubs, both in human and jaguar form, she almost lost count. With the sudden influx, she didn't know how Annabelle and Laura kept all the files straight and organized, but she adored them for their knowledge.

Then there were the pregnant females who craved the touch and assurance of a doctor instead of the ancient way of the older females who acted as midwives. One of those soon-to-be mothers was Hillary, who arrived with both her mates, for the last appointment of the day.

"Hello, Hillary. How are you feeling today?" Melinda stepped into the exam room and saw Hillary propped on the exam chair, which she could tilt back or extend as needed. She smiled to both males. "Hello again, Raphael, Sebastian."

"Hey, Doc," Sebastian said, continuing to hold Hillary's hand, while Raphael nodded.

"I'm doing well. Achy back and swollen feet, but I'm hanging in there. My boys are taking good care of me, even when I bitch at them. I'm glad Alex listened to my simple demands of opening the clinic," Hillary said with a chuckle.

"It's their job to take the bitching and hormones. I'm happy, too, that Alex listened to you and got me here," Melinda said with a wink.

"Okay. How about we lay you back and check out those cubs? You're expecting triplets, right?"

"I believe we are. The midwife heard the distinct heartbeats, but we're not sure. I feel feet and hands pushing, kicking, and playing with my bladder."

"How about we perform an ultrasound to check their progress?" Melinda hit the button on the chair to send it reclining back. "Just relax back against the cushion and let the seat do all the work."

"Oooh. I like this chair." Hillary wiggled in the chair as it rolled back.

"They are nice, aren't they?" Melinda went to Hillary's side and glanced at her mates. "Now, I need to touch her as a doctor. No freaking out with possessive growls. Otherwise both of you are banished to the waiting room."

"Umm. Okay. We'll behave," Sebastian said as he elbowed Raphael in his side to step back.

"*Si*, Doc, we'll behave," Raphael agreed.

Hillary chuckled with merciless glee. "How often do you say that?"

"Every time a tom comes in with his female. So annoying." Melinda lifted Hillary's shirt back to reveal the swollen belly.

"I look like I swallowed several basketballs. I can't believe I'm going to get bigger."

"You're perfectly fine, other than being stuffed with multiple fetuses that all need growing room. You'll most likely go early." Melinda moved her hands around the belly, feeling for the cubs. "Okay. I feel one cub up on the high left. Another over here on the right. And there is one down here by your bladder. This gel is cold." She squeezed some Aquasonic gel on Hillary's belly.

"Yikes. It's freezing," Hillary said.

"I know. I'm sorry." Melinda found the portable fetal heart monitor, placed the probe on one area, swished around the gel, and moved until she found the rapid fetal heartbeat. The unique *thump-thump-thump* filled the room. "There we go. Baby A's heartbeat."

"Oh wow. That's so cool," Sebastian said, his eyes going wide with awe.

"One of my favorite sounds as a doctor. Baby A sounds good, right on target for speed and beats. Let's go to Baby B. Ahh, here it is." Once again, the high thrumming sound of a tiny heart was heard.

"Oh, *mi carino*, how wondrous," Raphael said.

"And here is Baby C," Melinda said as she moved the probe to the lower belly with the gel. "Wait…"

"What? What is it?" Hillary asked.

"Something is odd. I'm hearing double heartbeats."

"Isn't it one of the other babies?" Sebastian asked. "Is everything okay?"

"Bastian, relax. I'm sure everything is fine," Hillary said to her worried mate. "Right, Doc?"

"Let me bring over the ultrasound machine, and we'll see what is happening. Be right back," Melinda said and stepped out of the room. Within a few minutes, she pushed a machine back into the room, plugged it in, twisted the monitor so the others could see, and calibrated it. She took up the large probe in one hand and placed it on Hillary's belly. "Okay. Let's see if we can find these cubs."

In a few seconds, Hillary and her mates made cooing sounds when they saw the side profile of a tiny face appear on the monitor. "Oh, how cute, we have a thumb-sucker!"

"Would you like to know the sexes?" Melinda printed a picture of the thumb-sucker with a note of Baby A on the print.

Hillary glanced at her mates, and everyone nodded.

"Okay. Let's see if they'll cooperate for us and give us a peek." Melinda moved the probe to change the view. "Baby A is a boy. See the little penis." She used a marker on the photo to show the men how they had a male baby.

"Wow. We start like that?" Sebastian asked.

Melinda chuckled and printed the second picture with the note of *I'm a boy!* She moved to Baby B and gave them a picture of the front view of the sweet face. "You have another boy," she said as she found the sex of the second baby. She captured another print with the same note.

"Two boys!" Raphael said and kissed Hillary.

"Now for this bottom triplet…" Melinda moved the wand around a few times. "Oh…Unexpected…" She changed the picture a few times until she was sure of the images.

"What? What is it?" Hillary asked.

"You're having twin girls. Identical twin girls, since they're in the same amniotic sac. You're having four cubs, Hillary. Congratulations."

"Twin girls? Wait… Four! I'm having four babies! I don't know what to do with one," Hillary said as her mouth dropped open.

"You do the same with one as you do with four. Just need a few more pairs of hands to hold them all, which you have," Melinda said with a chuckle.

Both males dropped to the floor in a dead faint.

"Uh-oh," Melinda said and laughed.

"Oh, great. Good going, boys!" Hillary shook her head as she stared at her mates. "They're going to be useless in the delivery room."

"I think it's a bit of a shock now. Common among toms." Melinda printed the last pictures of the twin girls and turned off the machine. She handed Hillary a cloth to wipe the gel off her belly. She stepped over the two males before she opened the door. "Nathan! Laura! I need a little help." She turned, planted hands on hips, and stared down.

"Unbelievable," Hillary said as she cleaned her belly, lowered her shirt, and moved as if to sit up.

"Hold on, let me move the chair," Melinda said as she hit the controls, and the chair lifted to its original position. "Now you have an extra story to tell the quads when they asked how their dads responded to the news." She reached out, grabbed the line of photos, ripped them from the printer, and handed Hillary the row. "Here's a little something for your baby book."

Hillary laughed. "Aww...Look at all these little faces. I can't believe the buggers stuffed me with four kids. I'm going to kill them."

"You love them to bits and would be lost without them."

"True. They did rescue me. I guess they can keep their heads for that reason alone."

Melinda patted Hillary's hand and chuckled. "I give you another month, maybe two until you deliver. They'll be small and will need a little help. I'll order some incubators and warmers to support them, but we'll give them the best care."

"I trust you." Hillary rubbed a hand over her swollen belly.

"Oh my...What happened?" Laura asked as Nathan burst into laughter when they entered the room.

"My idiot mates heard I was having four babies, not three. They fainted at the same time. Some big, brave guardians I have," Hillary said with a snort.

"They fainted?" Nathan said with his jaw dropped. "Umm. Congratulations on the big family."

"Out like a light," Melinda said.

"Ohhh...What happened?" Sebastian said as he came to.

"You fainted, you big idiot," Hillary said. "Four babies, remember?"

Sebastian placed a hand to his forehead and looked around. "I did what..."

"Fainted. Along with Raphael," Hillary repeated.

"I don't faint," Sebastian said.

"You did."

Sebastian smacked Raphael on his chest. "Wake up, amigo."

Raphael came to and stared around. "Where are we?"

"We're on the floor like a bunch of idiots. We both fainted," Sebastian said.

"*Oh mi diosa!*" Raphael rolled to a sitting position.

"Laura, Nathan, keep an eye on these two until they're stable." Melinda grabbed the folder and made a few notes. "Hillary, I need to see you once a week this next month and then twice a week to monitor the babies and their growth. If I decide later, you may be on permanent bed rest until you deliver to give their lungs time to mature. We need to keep you pregnant as long as possible, even for a jaguar mom."

"Okay," Melinda said.

"Same time as today?"

"Yes, it works for all three of us."

Melinda nodded and marked notes down. "I'm putting you on modified bed rest. I prefer you to sit or recline for most of the day either on the sofa or the bed. If possible, keep your feet elevated on a pillow. We want gravity working with us to keep those quads inside your womb. Keep trips up and down the stairs at a minimum. This means no working, no driving, and no household chores. You can get up long enough for bathroom visits, showers, and getting something to eat. Make sure you drink plenty of water throughout the day."

"No work? What about a laptop?"

"You can use it, but stay on the bed or sofa."

"Ugh. I'll be bored out of my mind."

"Get your boys to keep you occupied. Though…Watch it with the sex, please. Sex is known to induce labor, and we don't want that to happen."

"No sex?" Hillary groaned. "Boys, you're cut off."

"We heard," Sebastian grumbled.

Melinda shook her head. "Typical toms. Keep your meals light and small and snacks healthy. Instead of three big meals, split them up throughout the day. You'll need to increase the calorie intake, too."

"More food?"

"More babies, more calories used. How are you on your prenatal vitamins?"

"I have enough for another month. More water means more trips to the bathroom."

"I'm sorry, but it's part of the ordeal."

"Ugh."

"If this doesn't help, you'll have to stay here under strict hospital rest and IVs. I'm trying to avoid it for now."

"Me, too," Hillary said and rubbed her belly.

"We'll figure this out as we continue the pregnancy."

"Thanks, Doc."

"Give the boys time to recover, and you can go. I'll have Annabelle schedule the rest of your appointments and send you an email."

"Thanks, Doc Melinda, for everything."

"You're welcome, and congratulations on all four little ones," Melinda said as she chuckled while leaving. She headed down the hallway to Annabelle's office.

"What happened?" Annabelle said. "I heard loud thumps."

"Raphael and Sebastian fainted when I told them they're having quads, not triplets. Two boys and identical twin girls."

Annabelle cracked up laughing. "They fell to the floor?"

"Completely out," Melinda said with a snap of her fingers.

"Unbelievable. Of all the guardians, I wouldn't think they would drop."

"Hillary thinks they'll be useless for the delivery."

"Poor girl. She may be right."

"I have Laura and Nathan helping get them on their feet."

"Four babies?"

"One twin sister was hiding behind her sister, which is why no one heard her heartbeat. She moved today, so I could hear the double beats and confirmed with the ultrasound."

"Unbelievable. I'll alert the ladies to give her an extra-large baby shower. She's going to need everything."

"Yeah, she'll need a good-sized nursery at home with four of everything. Two boys and two girls. She's on modified bed rest at home so she'll not be able to do much in preparation."

"I'll make sure the ladies know and come to the house for her. They'll help prepare the nursery and keep her company."

"Good. I think she'll love the attention. Please schedule Hillary for this time for the next month and send her an email reminder."

"Will do. Anything else?"

"Yes. I have a feeling these quads will be premature, and we're not ready. We need to order radiant heat warmers, incubators, scales, physiologic monitors, bili lights, and all the other monitors and machines for premature infants and full-term infants. I want everything in place for the upcoming births. We have a lot of mothers coming due within the next month or two. Also order a transport incubator as a backup if a mom delivers at home and I need to run there for the delivery. I'll need something to keep the baby monitored."

"How much do you want me to order?" Annabelle pulled out a pad.

Melinda gave her all the numbers and listed out the equipment name and any other information to create a top-of-the-line NICU and nursery upstairs. "Plus, we'll need to make sure the room is glassed in and create an isolation system in place for the NICU."

"I'll get in the contractors to prepare both rooms within the week."

"Excellent. Order whatever you can this evening, and finish the list by tomorrow. I want everything delivered and set up within the next two weeks. For tonight, finish what you're doing and head home. Put the sign on the front doors to call my cell phone for emergencies. Laura and another nurse are taking the night rotation."

"Are you heading home then?"

"Yes, and Collin took Luca home yesterday. They said they had plans for a special night and I needed to come home on time."

"Enjoy, Doc. Happy mating night!"

Melinda blushed and nodded. "Thanks. Night, Annabelle."

"Night, Doc."

Chapter 14

Opening the front door to Collin's home, Melinda dropped her jaw at the wondrous sight before her. Candles flickered from every surface. White fairy lights sparkled everywhere else and even dangled from the ceiling. Bouquets of fragrant roses helped decorate everything. The finest parts stood at one end of the large living room—her two mates. They wore only jeans to reveal their mating bands on their arms and powerful chests. Each one held a long-stemmed rose.

"Collin...Luca...I'm overwhelmed. This is gorgeous." Melinda closed the door, dropped her bag on the nearest chair, and looked around. "What is all of this?"

"Welcome home, our mate. This is our first night together where we can celebrate as true mates," Collin said as he stepped forward, knelt, and presented the rose.

"First blessed and bound by our Goddess. Now we will be bonded with love and our bodies entwined," Luca said as he knelt next to Collin, his rose outstretched.

Melinda blushed, took the roses, and brought the large blooms close for a long sniff. "This is all so beautiful."

"As are you, our dearest beloved. This is a simple offering of our devotion and love." Collin rose to his feet. "There is more for us to show you." He offered his arm from her to take.

"We've been busy mates while you worked." Luca stood, having regained his fluid grace, and offered his arm on her other side.

"There is more than all this? How long did you plan this?" Melinda placed a hand on each of their arms. She lifted her face to accept a warm, loving kiss from each.

"Oh yes, much more," Luca said as his fingers graced a soft touch on her cheek. "Something you deserve every day of your life."

"We planned this night since we realized you were ours. Only, things took a little longer than we all wished," Collin said.

"Not like I meant to be attacked with a vicious poison," Luca said with a wry grin.

The men led her through the house, where she saw her personal things mixed within Collin's and Luca's items. Everything was displayed to reveal all of their styles and loves. She touched one of her paintings on the wall.

"I can't believe it. You unpacked everything," she said.

"We did, and we tried to place things together. You can rearrange whatever you like," Collin said. "My home is our home—yours, Luca's, and mine. I wanted it to reflect everyone."

"You moved in, too?" Melinda said to Luca.

"I asked Gideon and Alex to have all my things packed and moved the evening I woke and you stepped away for your rounds. Then this morning, I helped Collin rearrange everything."

"We had fun moving things around and figuring out what went with what," Collin said as they drew her to the kitchen, where delightful smells permeated. "Here…We have a special dinner waiting."

Melinda studied the waiting dishes and then said to her mates, "Can dinner hold a little longer or be reheated?"

"Yes, it'll be fine," Collin said with a glance at Luca.

"Good. Take me upstairs. I want both of you. No more waiting." She shifted her hands from their arms to their cheeks.

"We thought you would never ask." Luca moved to stand behind her, his chest pressed against her back until she could feel his erection nestled against her butt. He wrapped his arms around her.

"Luca, would you do the honors?" Collin asked.

"Love to," Luca said and scooped Melinda in his arms.

She let out a soft yip of surprise before winding her arms around his neck, her fingers sliding into his soft hair. She purred when Luca dropped his head and nuzzled her face.

Together, the males climbed the stairs and moved to the large master bedroom. When Collin opened the doors, Melinda gasped at the sight of more flickering candles and hundreds of roses scattered around.

"Did you get all the roses in the area?" she asked with a chuckle.

"Almost the state," Luca said. "Collin insisted on filling every nook and cranny with the flowers."

She laughed with delight.

"I have two mates I can indulge, cherish, adore, and show my eternal gratitude and love to for choosing me." Collin led them to the bed and found a bottle of lube from the nightstand. The covers were rolled back, and the bottom sheet was covered with velvety-soft petals.

Luca placed her on her feet next to the bed, and both men undressed her with gentleness and care. Luca was at her back with Collin in her front. They caressed, nipped, and licked every bit of skin revealed. When they dropped her pants, Collin moved his fingers against the lacy panty. His fingers found her drenched folds and captured some of her sweet cream.

"She's wet for us. So wet." Collin lifted his fingers to Luca, who tasted the wetness like a kitty with a bowl of cream.

"Delicious," Luca said with a moan. "I must try more."

"Indeed," Collin said as he helped Luca nudge down her panties until they fell to the floor.

Melinda gasped as both men lowered on their knees, encouraging her to open her legs wider. She moaned at the double sensation of warm breaths at her moist pussy. Someone's fingers opened the folds while another leaned in and sampled. Another's mouth opened to devour the rest of her. Her knees shook under the onslaught of pleasure. She dropped her hands to touch both of them.

Then one started suckling in earnest at her center, while the other used his fingers. First one finger slid inside and pumped, and then another joined the first, stretching her and adding to the delicious friction inside her pussy. She moaned and pulled in her lower lip as she nibbled.

"Oh, so good...There, right there...Oh, yes, please," she cried, encouraging them to continue the wonderful pleasure.

While one held her clit between his lips, tonguing it, the other pumped his fingers, finding her sensitive G-spot with ease. Together, they moved forward to drive her to the edge until she dropped her head back and screamed as she hit the shattering climax. Her body shivered and shuddered with pleasure. When she came down, her knees felt like Jell-O and collapsed, but two pairs of hands held her upright while they continued their mercilessness on her wet pussy. They managed to send her again and again into those incredible heights until she was so sensitive from their touch.

"Stop! Please, you must stop. I can't take anymore," she pleaded.

"Oh, you can take more. Much, much more from us." Luca kissed the length of her spine until he nipped her nape from behind.

"There is plenty more for us to show you." Collin nuzzled and kissed her breasts on his way back to his feet. "Oh, much more. Everything feels richer and more intense. I heard this is how things are between true mates." Collin lifted and deposited her on the bed. He settled between her legs, his cock pressing against her pussy, getting wet with her juices, and he propped himself on his elbows. He captured her lips in a long kiss.

Her fingers dove into his mahogany hair. She managed to hold the other toward Luca, who knelt next to them. She entwined her fingers with Luca's and held them.

"Are you ready to accept us as your mates?" Collin asked.

"Oh, yes. No more waiting," she said.

"Luca will enter me as I slide into your pussy."

"You don't want to prepare me?" Melinda said as she looked at Luca. "I'm willing to try both of you."

"Not this time. Luca and I will switch. We have plenty of time to learn what each other loves and desires the rest of our lives. Tonight is pleasure. Besides, I crave having Luca inside me." Collin glanced over his shoulder at their third. "I miss him."

"I missed you, my love." Luca kissed Collin then moved his lips to Melinda for another deep connection.

"Are you sure?" Melinda asked Luca, lifting her hand to cup his cheek.

"I am, my dearest. No matter how we take one another, we're connected." Luca leaned against her palm and nuzzled her skin before he kissed her fingers.

"I wanted to double-check," she said.

Luca grabbed the bottle of lube and knelt between their legs. He squeezed some lube on his fingers. "Darling, spread our handsome man's cheeks for me. I want you to play with us."

"With delightful pleasure," Melinda said as she smacked Collin's ass.

Collin yelped and purred. "Darling, do it again."

With a laugh, Melinda slapped his other cheek before she gave him a good grope.

"Hmm. I enjoyed that," he said as he stole a quick kiss.

Melinda took hold of his ass, massaged the wonderful muscle, and spread it to reveal the hidden opening to their lover. "How's this, Luca?"

"Ahh, what a perfect view of both of you," Luca said as he rubbed a slicked finger against Collin's hole.

Collin dipped his head against Melinda's chest and groaned. His purring increased when Luca slid two fingers inside him, a bit of pain and pleasure at the same time. He opened his thighs wider and pressed Melinda's legs further as he opened himself to the warm invasion. "More, Luca…"

Luca rubbed his thumb around the sensitive ring. His fingers made a scissor motion and thrust to open Collin. When he added a third finger, he pushed deeper to find the gland.

Collin moaned and rubbed his cock against Melinda's wet pussy. He growled as his hands gripped the sheets.

"What did you do?" Melinda asked.

"I got his prostate," Luca said as he nudged the gland again.

"I heard about the reaction…"

"No doctor-speak or reasoning, darling."

Melinda chuckled and kissed Collin's temple. "It's a habit."

"We know," Collin groaned. "Luca. Now, stop teasing. Get inside me."

"So bossy," Luca said as he slapped Collin's ass.

Collin groaned and rubbed his cock against Melinda, hitting her clit to make her moan.

Luca pulled his fingers out, used the extra lube on his cock, and held the flushed head to the prepared opening. He pushed forward, watching Collin's body open to accept him before the channel enclosed him in the delicious heat of a man's body. He pulled back and slid deeper into Collin.

Collin moaned, shuddered with pure pleasure, purred, and wiggled between them.

"Me…Come inside me," Melinda urged.

Luca lifted Collin's hips with one of his hands, kept himself deep inside, and guided Collin's cock to Melinda's moist pussy. "Wrap a leg around us, sweetheart," he said as his fingers moved and bumped her clit while he found the way.

Melinda lifted her leg and did as Luca asked. She tilted her head against the pillow as Collin's thick cock pushed deep inside her. She gripped Collin's waist with one hand, while her other found Luca's arm where he braced himself. "Oh, so good."

"Tell me about it." Collin kissed her neck. "Move us, Luca. Do it."

"It's time for a fast mating ride." Luca pulled them back and thrust forward. He drove inside Collin, forcing the cock buried deep inside Melinda to grind into her.

"Whatever, move!"

First it was slow, subtle lovemaking, which stimulated everyone's hypersensitive nerves. There was the gentle drag and pull within both of them. The friction built between the three of them, causing them all to moan and elicit more responses.

There was ragged breathing, groans, and moans as they moved together in the ancient rhythm. Absolute desire and ecstasy surrounded them.

"Not going to last…" Collin groaned.

It caused Luca to drive faster and harder into Collin, which drove him long and deep into Melinda. She tensed when Collin nudged her clit. Luca picked up their rhythm once more until she shattered around Collin. She called out their names.

Collin followed her over the edge, shooting pulses of cum deep inside her body. His ass squeezed around Luca's cock. His cock flexed and pulsed with her contractions.

Luca groaned and sank his teeth into Collin's nape as his cock released ropes of pearly cum inside their lover.

Melinda thought her orgasm felt endless when Collin bit her, causing her to lift into another wave. Her fingernails dug into both of them.

"Ahh, damn, you're still coming," Collin moaned.

Luca was careful when he pulled out of Collin's ass. He licked his bite marks closed on Collin's skin. He dropped to one side of them, exhausted and covered in sweat.

Collin latched onto her mouth for a kiss as she finished squeezing his cock. Then he withdrew from her. He lowered on the other side, which placed her in the middle.

Melinda turned his head and captured Luca's mouth in a kiss. It was searing as Luca held onto the back of her neck to hold her close. When he let her go, she dropped her head to the pillow and closed her eyes. "You two exhaust me. I feel so wonderful."

"Sleep in our arms, love. We're going nowhere." Collin curled against one side, wrapped an arm around her waist, and placed his fingers on Luca.

Luca reached to a nightstand for baby wipes they hid there. He cleaned Collin's ass. He used a different one for himself. Using a feminine wipe, he took care of Melinda.

With a little yawn, Melinda snuggled next to Collin. She felt Luca's warm weight against her back, managed to join their hands, and slid deeper into sleep. Then her cell phone rang loud from the pile of clothes. The urgent tone repeated.

"What the hell?" Collin murmured.

"Phone. Tone. Clinic," she muttered, pushing a hand on his shoulder to rise and find the phone. Melinda propped herself on an elbow, knuckling the sleep from her eyes.

"This is what it means to be mated to a doctor," Luca said as Collin rolled out of bed and dug through the pile of clothes. He rose to watch Collin unearth the phone and turn it on.

"Collin here. Who is this?" he grumbled.

"Collin..." Melinda said.

"It's our mating night. Can't you handle it?"

"Collin!" Melinda slapped his arm and made a *gimme* motion with her fingers.

"Oh! Crap. Guess not...Umm, here's Melinda." Collin turned and held out the phone. "It's Laura. A jaguar female is in the clinic and ready to give birth, but there's trouble. One of the cubs is turned."

"A breech baby? Oh no," she said and took the phone. "Laura, talk to me." She rolled out, held the phone to her ear with her shoulder, and searched for clothes.

Realizing what she was doing, Luca moved from bed and went to where they placed her clothes. He pulled out underwear, a bra, an undershirt, and fresh scrubs. He laid the clothing on the bed and tapped her shoulder.

Melinda turned and saw the clothes. She mouthed "thank you" and dressed. She felt someone's fingers in her hair when she stopped. Since Luca was in front, tugging on a pair of pants, she realized it was Collin, who combed and braided the long locks with ease. She grabbed and kissed his fingers.

"Are you on your way?" Laura asked over the phone. "Felicia is afraid and is struggling not to push."

"Yeah, I'm on my way." Melinda followed her men downstairs, pushed her feet in the waiting Crocs, grabbed her bag, and saw Luca reaching for her keys. "Don't let her push. I need to assess the situation. Keep her in the breathing exercises for another five minutes."

"Okay. We're in the back treatment room in case you decide a C-section is best."

"Good. I'll be right there." Melinda took her keys and kissed her men's cheeks. "I'm sorry to ruin our mating night. I must go."

Luca shrugged. "We understand. It's part of being mated to a doctor."

"I love both of you. Somehow we'll get an entire night for ourselves," she said.

"Go. Go. You have babies to deliver," Luca said.

"Come home when you can," Collin said. "We love you, too."

With a grin, Melinda raced away from her lovers to attend a difficult birth. Her body tingled from their lovemaking and energized her to face anything that could come her way. Seeing both her men in the door as she drove away, Melinda knew they would be there when she came home, and it was the best feeling in the world.

She never wanted to forget that image.

THE END

WWW.NICOLEDENNISAUTHOR.COM

ABOUT THE AUTHOR

Ever the quiet one growing up, Nicole Dennis often slid away from reality and curled up with a book to slip into the worlds of her favorite authors. Since then, she's had a fascination with fantasy, paranormal and the never-ending appeal and beauty of romance. It seems only natural all of these loves would come together in her writing from simple stories for her dolls until the summer when her aunt introduced her to romance novels. What a world opened.

It's been non-stop since hot New Jersey summer. It's only gotten worse (in a good way). Now she's created a personal library full of novels filled with dragons, fairies, vampires, shape-shifters of all kinds, and romance. Always she returned to romance. Still, there were these characters in her head, worlds wanting to be built on paper, and stories wanting to be told and she began writing them down whether during or after class. She continues to this day. Only recently has it begun to become fruitful, spreading out to let others read and enter her worlds, meet her characters, and see what she sees. No matter what she writes, her stories of romance with their twists of paranormal, fantasy, and erotica will always have their Happily Ever Afters.

She currently works in a quiet office in Central Florida, where she also makes her home, and enjoys the down time to slip into her characters and worlds to escape reality from time to time. At home, she becomes human slave to a semi-demonic black-orange calico.

She loves to hear from readers and fans, so don't be shy. Find her on the 'net or send an email. Find her at the following links:

www.facebook.com/#!/pages/Nicole-Dennis/107177776016259
www.twitter.com/Nicole_Dennis
nicoledennis.author@gmail.com

For all titles by Nicole Dennis, please visit
www.bookstrand.com/nicole-dennis

Siren Publishing, Inc.
www.SirenPublishing.com

CPSIA information can be obtained at www.ICGtesting.com
Printed in the USA
LVOW12s1953140514

385785LV00027B/1295/P